THE LEMON GROVE

Caroline Beaumont splits from her fiancé and is made redundant in one fell swoop. Her brother Oscar offers her an escape to the beautiful area of Sorrento in Italy. But she is thrown into confusion when Antonio, a local hotelier's son, falls for her. And then Antonio's wayward sister disappears . . . Is his family a victim of an old enemy with connections to the Mafia? Caroline will come to understand that in Italy, *la famiglia* — the family, with all its joys and problems — means absolutely everything.

CARA COOPER

THE LEMON GROVE

Complete and Unabridged

LINFORD
Leicester

First published in Great Britain in 2013

First Linford Edition
published 2015

A catalogue record for this book is available
from the British Library.

ISBN 978–1–4448–2333–2

Published by
F. A. Thorpe (Publishing)
Anstey, Leicestershire

Set by Words & Graphics Ltd.
Anstey, Leicestershire
Printed and bound in Great Britain by
T. J. International Ltd., Padstow, Cornwall

This book is printed on acid-free paper

1

Caroline Beaumont remembered she wasn't in England when she woke to a cockerel crowing and blazing sunlight squeezing underneath the heavy hotel curtains. It had been tipping with rain in London, but here in Sorrento April sun was already warming the Italian earth.

She wasn't looking forward to today. This was no ordinary holiday, and her planned trip into Naples wasn't for pleasure as she'd heard the city was busy with crowds, traffic and mayhem. Oscar, her brother, was due to holiday out here with them but had been delayed by a crisis at work. So he had asked her to do a favour. Dear Oscar had been so good to her over the past difficult months, she couldn't say no.

A gentle knock shook the door. 'Auntie Caro, are you awake?'

Caroline's niece Isobel was only fourteen, young enough to be excited by anything and everything, and especially by her first morning in a foreign hotel. Caroline felt a jolt as her feet struck the chilly tiles. The Italian spring was warm in the day, but still only eleven degrees this early. Gathering her cotton wrap around her, she opened the door.

Izzy crashed into the room like a skinny whirlwind, yanked apart the French windows, then the green shutters to the balcony. 'Oh, I'm going to love it here. When will we get to see the beach house, Auntie Caro? Daddy's a real star to buy a hideaway so we can have proper family holidays again. I hope he gets here soon. Are you going to get the keys to the beach house today?'

Caroline's heart lurched. Izzy had done so well in her short life to conquer sadness with hope. 'Heavens.' Caroline sank back onto the bed and breathed in the crisp air filtering into the room.

2

'You make me dizzy with so many questions first thing. I need breakfast and coffee to get my head together. We should get to see the house later today — *La Casa di Spiaggia*, the house on the beach. It does sound wonderful.'

They gazed out at the dew-soaked lemon grove below. Caroline put an arm around the girl, feeling protective towards her. She hoped to goodness this holiday was everything Izzy wished for. The beach in Marina di Paulo, a tiny cove, was reputedly one of the best on the Amalfi coast. Caroline thought of her older brother Oscar. He deserved some good luck. He had experienced more heartache in the past two years than many people do in a lifetime. He'd been buried too much in his work lately, but it was a means to forget and she couldn't begrudge him that. It was typical, though, of Oscar to put Izzy first. This beach house idea of his was to give him a chance to get right away from his job as a hotshot London lawyer, so he could dedicate time to

Izzy. Time she desperately needed now she only had one parent. Losing her mother to cancer had been tough.

Caroline thought back to that cold day in January when Oscar had phoned, inviting her out with Izzy. Izzy was fond of art and visiting galleries. 'We're going to have lunch at the Tate but also we've got some news, and Izzy wants to be the first to tell you.'

'Sounds lovely.' Caroline was pleased at the excitement she'd detected in Oscar's voice. 'See you at the entrance at noon.'

Since his wife Louise's untimely death, Oscar had been too preoccupied with work and she hoped maybe their news involved him getting some normality back into his life. As they waved to her across the rain-spattered trees outside the art gallery Caroline was pleased to see that Izzy wasn't too old to be holding her father's hand. The three of them kissed and hugged, then Oscar said, 'Which bit of the gallery first, Izzy? You choose.'

'How about the café? I'm thirsty. I can tell Auntie Caro our news over drinks. Then we can go and look at the new photography gallery.'

Hugging a hot chocolate, looking out at the Thames, Caroline said: 'Okay, so what's up? The suspense is killing me!' Izzy had grinned conspiratorially at her father. Bursting with the news, her pixie face was brighter than Caroline had seen it in ages.

'Daddy's bought a tiny house on a beach in Italy through something called an internet auction. It needs painting, but I can help with that. Daddy's going to let me choose the colour scheme.' Caroline had looked quizzically at Oscar.

'Well, Caroline, you're unusually quiet. Say something.'

'An internet auction sounds intriguing. But you haven't visited the house?'

'I was due to go, but something at work blew up and I couldn't make it before the auction. But it's fine. I had the place checked out by a friend.'

Caroline smiled weakly. Goodness knows, she didn't want to dampen Oscar's spirits, but she was ultra-cautious whereas Oscar was a risk-taker. As they had finished their drinks and Izzy was keen to go and see the new exhibition, they walked downstairs. The photographic gallery with its floor-to-ceiling windows was bright despite the rain outside.

'Don't frown at me, Caroline,' said Oscar as they strolled past the exhibition. 'I did arrange to nip out to Italy for the weekend before the auction but had to cancel it.'

'Work again?' Caroline scowled.

'As it happens, a friend offered to have a look for me while he was out there visiting relatives at Christmas. He said it's a great place. Here, I've printed you out the photographs, what do you think?'

Caroline's doubts dissolved as she flicked through the images. 'Oh, it's gorgeous.' The neat whitewashed house dripped with jasmine and wisteria. The interior was a dull blue but looked sound and simply needed brightening up.

'Isn't it? Besides, you can't go wrong on that coastline. The house is an old boat repairer's place. A lick of paint and some new shutters should sort it out. There's a small marina and a couple of restaurants. It's becoming a haunt for yachts touring the bay of Naples who want to avoid the busy parts of Sorrento. It's a steal, and Izzy's already fallen in love with it.'

Izzy broke off from peering at the exhibition photos. 'It's an investment for my future. Daddy says maybe one day it will pay my university fees if we rent it out. But for now we're going to enjoy it. Daddy's buying me a new camera which works underwater so I can practise my photography.'

'I was hoping you might do me a favour, Caroline.'

'What's that?' Caroline had asked.

'Well, when you told me you were being made redundant, I wondered if you would come out to Italy with us at Easter and help me and Izzy paint the place. You girls could choose curtains and stuff, it could be fun.' His eyes willed her to say yes. Oscar's wife had been an interior designer, and Caroline felt a pang as she realised Oscar didn't have the heart to do that sort of thing on his own. 'I'd pay for your flights, we could hire a car and look around the area a bit. What do you say? It would be great to do while Izzy's off school. Besides it'll give you a focus. Take your mind off . . . ' He hesitated. ' . . . things, until your new job starts after the summer.'

Oscar was only trying to help. Caroline's life had reached a cross-roads. A recent love affair had ended badly, and on top of that, she had been made redundant. She wasn't due to start her new job until the autumn and her redundancy money was tiding her over. Perhaps some time away would give her the change of scenery she needed.

Izzy's voice had dragged her out of her reverie. 'Are you coming to Italy with us at Easter, Auntie Caro? It would be cool to all go away together.' Caroline looked at the rain spattering the window and her mind was made up.

'Of course I will, it sounds lovely — even if your father is going to use me as cheap labour!' Caroline laughed and was delighted to see Oscar's smile of relief.

So here she was, finally starting her Easter adventure in Italy. Thinking back to those cold winter months, and her recent difficulties, Caroline sighed. But she forced her thoughts back to the present as Izzy looked up at her with wide blue eyes. 'Are you okay, Auntie Caro?'

'Of course I am, I'll be fine once I've been into Naples and picked up the keys.'

'Why can't I come too?'

'Because it'll be boring for you at the estate agent's. We'll set aside another day and see some of the sights properly.

Besides, I want you to do something far more important.' She cupped Izzy's pale face in her hands. 'It's your Dad's birthday very soon and I didn't have a chance to pick him up a present in London. It would be lovely to get something very special and Italian for the new house to thank him for this lovely holiday. If you and Mel go into Sorrento and take a good look around, I can pop back with you tomorrow and pick it up.' Izzy brightened at the thought. Like all teenagers she loved shopping. Then her pretty face wrinkled in a frown.

'You're not driving in Naples, are you, Auntie Caro? The roads are terribly busy over here.' Losing her mother so early had left the child overprotective of those close to her. What Izzy needed, thought Caroline, as she gazed on the child's serious face, was more fun. Oscar had done the right thing in buying the beach house. It was going to be idyllic.

'No, I wouldn't risk driving over here

yet. Those roads with sheer drops into the sea would be a challenge. I'm going over by ferry. You and Mel can see me off at the port in Sorrento and then another day, I'll take you over on the ferry to Capri. That's meant to be lovely, with beautiful flowers.'

'Will you be long in Naples?'

'No. I'll be back by late afternoon.'

Caroline could see Izzy weighing this information and knew she wouldn't be happy until her aunt returned safely. Caroline often wondered about Oscar's priorities. He worked like a Trojan to send Izzy to private school, but what she really needed was people to spend time with her. Preferably her father and possibly a mother substitute. True, Oscar couldn't produce a mother for Izzy out of thin air, but Caroline hadn't taken to the few girlfriends he'd had since. They'd all been career lawyers — too ambitious to care for a stepdaughter.

Caroline chided herself. She couldn't know what it was like to lose the love of your life because she had never found that special person, whereas poor Oscar had . . . and had lost her. Much of his limited leisure time he spent with Izzy. Caroline pondered whether, ironically, his devotion to his daughter prevented him finding a new wife, or whether he was simply too scared to take the plunge again . . .

Caroline stepped out onto the balcony and brushed her hair. If only she could sort out the knots of Oscar's life — and her own — that easily. Izzy's hand stole into hers as they stood breathing in the citrus blossom scent. 'See Izzy, that's the bay of Paulo in the distance.' A blue morning haze settled over the calm sea. 'Is Mel up yet?' Melinda Sanderson, Izzy's nanny, had been with the family since Izzy was a baby and Oscar had kept her on as an invaluable helper and housekeeper.

'Yes, she's in the shower.'

'Good, I must get showered too, and then we'll go down to breakfast. Are you hungry?'

'Starving.'

'Okay. Race you.' Izzy disappeared off into her own room at breakneck speed leaving Caroline with nothing but the gentle ring of birdsong and the distant clatter of breakfast things being got ready in the dining room.

★　★　★

As Nello knocked the jasmine plant out of its pot and placed it into the hole Antonio had dug, he broke the morning's silence. 'It was good of your father to give me this work at the hotel, Antonio.'

Antonio wiped his forehead with the back of his hand. Although in the shade of the trees it was cool, here near the hotel swimming pool in the sun the two friends had already worked up a sweat.

'No worries.' Antonio shrugged off his friend's thanks in his easy Neapolitan way, pushing back the mop of dark brown hair settling on his forehead. 'It was about time my father revitalised this garden. Guests expect more than a few lemon trees nowadays. You're a good plantsman, Nello. I remember when we were at school together, you bringing flowers for the teacher at Easter when we were all plying her with chocolate eggs. She always preferred your flowers.'

'Maybe,' chuckled Nello. Then, as if he were discussing the weather, rather than the vital matter of what two young men were going to do with their futures, he said: 'Antonio, I'm still looking for a partner for my business. There's a place for you. I might be great with plants but I hate accounts. Book learning was always your thing. If you're still hoping to avoid having to follow your father into the hotel business, it could be a way out.'

Antonio grinned, stood up, brushing the dark volcanic soil off his fingers, and stretched his back. 'Good try, Nello my friend, I'm flattered by your faith in me. But I'm as interested in gardening as I am in the hotel trade. In other words, not at all. I'm sorry, but the answer is 'no', the same as the last time you asked. You're as bad as my father; he only let me do that archaeology degree because he thought I'd get bored with it and end up wanting to work in the hotel, but he just doesn't understand. He's always trying to sort out my future.' Antonio felt a stab of guilt and winced at the familiar sign of disappointment on his friend's face. He could have run Nello's business easily, likewise his father's hotel, but had no inclination to do either. He wondered whether he was destined to disappoint people at every turn. At least he could be straight with Nello. It was more difficult when Antonio was speaking to his father. Salvatore was of the old school. In the stern older man's world, sons loyally followed their fathers into lucrative businesses — why wouldn't they? Antonio had tried to tell Salvatore a hundred times that he was not going to take over the 'Hotel Girasole'. But somehow Antonio couldn't be direct

15

with his father as he could with his friend.

He could see his proud father in his mind's eye, thick brows knitted like an eagle, arms crossed in front of him, whether he was overseeing the scurrying staff as they kept the hotel in order or whether he was standing in judgement on his son.

Antonio shook thoughts of his father's disapproving gaze out of his mind. He just wanted to enjoy this fabulous morning and Nello's easy company. 'Can I get you an orange juice, Nello?'

Nello nodded, sweat dripping off his forehead. Antonio unlocked the door to the poolside bar to raid the fridge. It was, he thought, tipping juice into two glasses, one of the few benefits of being the proprietor's son that he could take what he wanted, when he wanted. Although he would still have to pay for their drinks. Salvatore ran the 'Girasole' like a finely-oiled military operation.

'*Salute!*' They drank, glad of a break.

Lula, the hotel's black and white cat, strolled across the grass, then pounced on a bunch of bright purple Cape daisies whose opening petals lazily greeted the morning sun. 'Hey, shoo, Lula.' Antonio strode over on long legs scooping up the cat who nuzzled into his chin. '*Gatto matto*, you'll end up getting stung chasing bees like that.' He held her like a baby, rubbing her tummy until she purred. Chuckling, he deposited her under the shade of an orange tree and beckoned to Nello. 'Come on friend, only two more jasmines to plant, then you can tend to the geraniums and I can get off to my books.'

'Books, books, that's all you think about. You'll make no money. The worst thing that ever happened to you was winning this darned archaeology fellowship. Why on earth anybody should pay you to dig up more old pottery is a mystery to me. Italy's already overflowing with the stuff. Besides, archaeology's no job for a young man, you should leave it to the grey old Professore.' Nello whisked up another jasmine plant and Antonio caught its heady sweet scent.

'Perhaps, but if I'm lucky I'll soon be helping to discover the secrets of the last temples unearthed at Pompeii. I'm off to see the Professore this afternoon. Only some of his students are chosen to help with the important digs. How can you live in a place like this and not feel the ancient world in the soil?' Antonio's passion shone like the golden specks in his eyes, which were the colour of dark sun-ripened olives.

'No, Antonio, I live for now. Yesterday's dead and buried and it should stay that way.'

'Philistine.' Antonio cuffed Nello playfully on the chin and it was like they were two schoolboys again. 'Well, as far as I'm concerned, the ancients have more life in them than this dull old hotel. What's more, it may be my father's wish for me to go into the family business but my mother's always encouraged me to follow my dreams. Maybe she'll be the one person on earth I don't disappoint. You get on with planting and I'll go off and get the hosepipe to water them in.'

'That's it, book-learner, you take the light work and I'll do the heavy stuff,' joked Nello as Antonio marched off.

Antonio was glad to be round the back of the hotel away from the sun. As he turned the tap on, he heard it splutter and cough with the hose hiccupping instead of sending out a satisfying gush. '*Mamma mia*,' Antonio muttered. That was the dratted thing about hotel management, something was forever going wrong. Antonio's stomach rumbled like a creaking door; he wanted his breakfast badly, but if he left those jasmine plants to bake without water they'd die in a day. Peeved, he marched off to go and fix the problem, once again making the vow that he would soon face up to his father and tell him he was quitting the hotel. Salvatore might be happy to be

Girasole's slave as well as its master, but Antonio was determined never to be trapped like that.

★   ★   ★

'Isn't this a beautiful dining room, full of morning sun,' exclaimed Mel as the waiter deposited a steaming coffee at her place. Izzy was up helping herself to the array of goodies spread on the buffet. 'How are you doing, Caroline?'

It was in Mel's nature to look after everyone. She collected people like a mother cat collects her kittens. She wasn't just a nanny to Izzy, she'd become a good friend to Caroline. Recently Caroline had found Mel scrutinising her when she thought she wasn't looking, for telltale signs of lines appearing on her forehead or shadows under her eyes. 'I'm fine thanks, Mel.' She reached out and squeezed her friend's hand. 'You mustn't worry about me. I've got a good feeling about this holiday, it's a fresh start for all of us. I hope Oscar can make it here soon. I sometimes feel that Izzy misses out by having a talented successful father. He's always tired. Now he's a single parent he's so conscious of providing for her, he's torn both ways.'

'I know,' Mel sighed. 'But we don't always choose the hand we're given do we? Oscar's heart's in the right place.'

'I know. It hasn't been easy for him.'

Izzy came back carrying a side plate piled with strawberries. 'They've got a fab spread. There's everything you'd want, even this cool machine where you put in your bread and it goes on a conveyor and comes out toasted. And there's scrambled eggs and sausages like the ones you have on sticks and cereal and juice and . . . ' She paused to take breath before sitting down and stuffing a huge strawberry into her mouth. ' . . . well, everything.'

Caroline laughed. 'As long as you eat all the food you put on your plate that's okay. With buffets you have to be careful. It can be tempting to get carried away because things are sitting there to be taken. But it's a sin to take stuff and not eat it.'

'I won't, I promise.' With that, Izzy was off to try out the toasting machine, as one of the waiters showed her how to use it.

'It's wonderful to see her eating. She's so skinny, I worry about her.'

'You and me both,' agreed Mel. 'You've lost weight too, Caroline. I recommend that good old Italian diet of pasta, pizza and lashings of delicious ice cream. I was talking to the man on reception and he says Sorrento has the best ice cream parlour on this coast. There are over a hundred flavours, everything from apricot to zabaglione — whatever that is. We'll soon have you glowing with health again.'

'You mustn't worry about me, I'm fine really. But breaking off an engagement is such a major thing. I do often wonder if I made the right decision. Besides, my friends are getting married — I've got three weddings to go to this year. And some are having children. It's lonely up here on the shelf.'

'Nonsense. You're too pretty to stay on the shelf for long. You were brave to call the wedding off. Many girls wouldn't have the courage, and many have lived to regret going through a marriage they knew in their hearts wasn't right.'

Just talking about her ex-fiancé had made Caroline's chest tighten in that old familiar stress reaction. She had loved him very much in the beginning. Would she ever find anyone to make a future with?

Izzy slid back into her place with three slices of toast, jam and marmalade. 'Izzy, you're never going to eat all of those.'

'I will, I promise. I was going to take four slices then I remembered what you said. I do like toast, you know.'

'Yes, I know,' smiled Caroline, and got up to go and help herself to scrambled egg. As she lifted the lid on the large metal chafing dish, she heard one of the waitresses chatting with the head waiter, who was English, and was standing ready in case anyone wanted tea or coffee. 'And how are you this morning, Sophia?'

'Well enough,' came the petulant reply. Caroline had been struck by the woman's dark beauty, her careful hairdo and makeup. Caroline got the impression the waitress felt her job was beneath her.

'Come on Sophia, it's still early in the season, so at least we get the chance to stand around and chat a little before the big rush begins.'

Sophia threw her hands up. 'For us women life is constant work. Before I came in for my shift, I had already done an hour in my garden. And why is it all my beautiful roses insist on flowering on the other side of the fence? I waste hours tying them back.'

'In England, Sophia, we have a phrase which goes, 'The other man's grass is always greener'. I think probably things just seem that way to you. We're lucky both to have jobs, and that the Hotel Girasole is doing good business.'

The waitress flounced off to attend to a guest. Caroline had to smile. That was one of the interesting things about holidays — having the time to observe other people. Everyone had their problems, but hopefully Caroline's seemed to be over.

'Those eggs look good,' said Mel as Caroline arrived back at their table. 'So, when are you off to Naples?'

'I don't have to leave until 11.00 am so I'll sit around the pool and read my book. I've brought it down in my bag. The water's probably a bit chilly for you to swim yet, Izzy, but if you want to get your costume on and join me you can try.'

'Okay.'

Once they had finished eating, Caroline wandered out. At the back of the pool was a gate leading to a small garden. As she was about to open the gate, she saw a solid, squat young gardener with large feet and heavy boots, firming down some plants. Then, she saw another gardener, in his mid-twenties like herself, tall and incredibly good-looking in a dark Italian way, with an unruly fringe which he kept scraping off his forehead. Slim-hipped, he carried a hose over to his colleague. She was mesmerised by his big cat walk and by the laughter lines playing around his mouth, betraying a sense of fun. She nearly laughed out loud as he playfully sprayed his partner with a jet of water.

Caroline had an insane wish to go and join the two gardeners in their simple occupation. Everything seemed trouble-free inside the garden. She longed to go in and forget memories of her cancelled wedding and worries about her trip to Naples, which tumbled around her mind like clothes whirling in a washing machine. She glanced up and caught the dark-haired, slimmer of the two gardeners, hands on hips, looking at her with interest. His gaze was bold, not insolent but steady and appreciative. She found her cheeks burning crimson. Caroline had heard Italian men were direct but such openness embarrassed her. Besides, memories of her fiancé were still too raw.

Caroline walked back to the pool and took out her book. But, although she looked at the pages, none of the words went in.

'Hi.' There was Izzy in a bathing robe. 'Mel has said she'd be happy taking me shopping for Daddy's present after lunch. Apparently Sorrento's full of cool shops and she's going to buy me a new bikini too. I've almost grown out of this old costume.' Mel came over to join them and the three of them spent a pleasant morning until it was time for Caroline to leave.

Caroline enjoyed the ferry ride. Gathering clouds reflected in the azure sea making her think that the weather could go either way today, possibly sun, possibly rain. As the ferry docked into the port teeming with people stepping on and off boats, the world's largest traffic jam deafened her with tooting, hooting cars bumper to bumper. She had to skip sharply aside when a screeching scooter careered up on the pavement to avoid the traffic jam, before dropping back on the road without anyone batting an eyelid. It seemed that Neapolitans were as reckless as she had heard.

Keen to be on time for her appointment, Caroline had arrived much earlier than need be. So, quickly checking in her guidebook for an eatery near to the estate agent's, she hailed a taxi and asked to be taken there for lunch. The family-run restaurant was noisy with students from the nearby college buildings. Caroline had to chuckle to herself when the *quattro stagioni* pizza she ordered was so huge it hung over the sides of the plate. Whilst she struggled to eat half of hers, the chattering students demolished theirs with no problem. She marvelled at how Italians talked as much with their hands as with their voices.

When Caroline left, she judged the estate agent's office to be only five minutes' walk. She belted her jacket tightly against the chill, for the bright sun had disappeared and been replaced with ugly clouds. Hurrying now, it was ten minutes before she realised she had walked backwards down the *Via dei Tribunali* and had taken a wrong turn into the tangled maze of alleys. Before she knew it, she had lost her bearings completely. Washing flapped in the wind, strung out between the balconies of dirty grey buildings like mismatched bunting. Caroline could have kicked herself for relying on a silly tourist map which had only the main roads and none of the side streets. People scurried past her and spots of cold rain were now making the large cobblestones slippery underfoot.

Hurrying to avoid the shower, and concentrating on putting up the hood of her jacket, she slipped, dropping her handbag and squealing as she watched the entire contents fly over the cobbles. That was the last thing she needed. When all of a sudden, a man's voice — in excellent English, but with an engaging Italian lilt — said, 'Please, allow me.'

Caroline peered from under her hood to see the gardener she had noticed this morning at the Girasole. He had no mud on his hands now, which were scrubbed clean with a gold signet ring on his little finger. He wore cream-coloured chinos and a blue designer shirt. A smart leather man-bag over his shoulder rested on his hip. He had been walking with a group of friends who skittered out of the rain, calling *'Ciao!'* and waving him goodbye as he knelt down to help Caroline collect the detritus from her handbag. He ran after the inadequate map that fluttered away in the wind and she grabbed at rolling pens and lipgloss. He came to her side saying, 'I hope you do not mind my helping, but you looked very lost.

Napoli can be a confusing city.'

Embarrassed, Caroline said, 'I've been foolish, I'm afraid. I thought I could navigate easily but that map really wasn't up to the job.'

'Don't blame yourself. With every other street in Napoli being Via San this or Vico San that, we're often helping tourists who are lost. And this rain doesn't help. Permit me.' He extended a hand to beckon her into a doorway with a canopy under which they could shelter. Already she felt better. His was such a friendly smile and so, so handsome she had to try hard not to stare. Now that they were face to face and she had tipped off her hood, he quirked an eyebrow and said, 'Correct me if I am wrong but I believe you are staying at The Girasole Hotel; did I not see you there this morning?'

Caroline blushed. 'You're right, I am staying at the hotel with my niece and a friend. Thank you so much for your help. I'm terribly late, I'm heading for an estate agent's office. I should be there in ten minutes but I'm miles away.'

He scrutinised the letter she handed him. 'Your sense of direction is better than you thought. We can walk it in five minutes — if, that is, you do not mind accompaniment.'

'I would be very, very happy for accompaniment.' It was partly relief, and partly Caroline's acute sense of humour which made her giggle — he had sounded as if he was about to take out a guitar and accompany her in a song.

'I have said something funny?' His eyebrow raised and his tanned face looked bemused. 'I like to improve my English; please tell me if I made a mistake.'

'Only a tiny one, and it's a bit difficult to explain, but I'll try as we walk if you don't mind.'

He unfurled an umbrella from his bag, and Caroline was acutely aware of his aftershave — sandalwood and spice as he sheltered her from the rain.

Chatting was easy and she found herself telling him about the reason for her trip into Naples and how excited Izzy would be when they finally saw the *Casa di Spiaggia*. With his long confident strides they made the estate agent's in no time. 'Forgive me,' he said when they arrived in the foyer. 'I haven't even formally introduced myself. Antonio Marco di Labati, at your service.' He held out a hand. His fingers closed around hers, warm and inviting.

'Caroline Beaumont,' she smiled, wishing that the gentle Neapolitan rain hadn't started to make her unruly blonde hair curl. 'Your English is good. I'm afraid my Italian is hopeless.'

'Thank you. I studied in England briefly, at University College London. And now, we are here.' He hesitated. There was a pause as if he didn't yet want to leave her. 'I wonder, I have over an hour before I go to catch the ferry back to Sorrento. If you might want someone to show you the way back, or if you might need someone to help translate when you meet the estate agent, I would be happy to stay.'

One of the reasons she had been apprehensive about her visit today was in case the estate agent might have given her documents for Oscar that she might not understand. This man's offer was attractive in more ways than one.

'Are you sure you have the time, Mr di Labati?'

'Please call me Antonio,' he corrected her. 'In fact you would be doing me a kindness. If I don't stay here in this nice dry office I shall have to go out in the rain again and sit in the library at the university. I have had enough studying for today and enough of getting wet. I would be very happy to help, if I can.'

But when they were ushered into the office, Caroline thought the estate agent looked uneasy. 'Please take a seat. Signorina Beaumont, Signor di Labati, I am afraid I have some difficult news for you. I really do not know how to tell you. It is about *La Casa di Spiaggia*.'

'Difficult news? Do you not have the keys for some reason?' Caroline could see that it was something much worse than that. The poor man looked ragged, with beads of sweat breaking out on his forehead. If only he would stand still and not pace up and down behind his desk in that distracting way. His voice broke as he finally took a deep breath and looked her in the eye.

'If only it were as simple as that. I cannot find an easy way to tell you this. But I am afraid your brother has been the victim of fraud; and not just your brother, but also my firm.'

'Why, what's happened?'

'The man who negotiated with your brother, one of our employees, has been found to have been misappropriating funds. He has disappeared with a large amount of money. Not only that, but he has been marketing the wrong properties to overseas clients and pocketing the profits.' He pushed a photo towards her. 'This is *La Casa di Spiaggia*.'

Caroline felt waves of nausea engulf

her and if she hadn't been sitting down, would surely have collapsed. She and Antonio leaned forward to see a building that was not the neat white and blue house from Oscar's photograph. This house was very similar in size and shape, but that was all. A massive hole gaped in the roof, neglected window shutters dangled by jagged broken glass and a tangle of greenery invaded the crumbling brickwork like a disease.

'But — but — ' Caroline slapped her hand to her mouth. She struggled to find words, whilst Antonio motioned to the estate agent to fetch her a glass of water. 'What in heaven's name am I going to tell Oscar, and how on *earth* am I going to tell poor Izzy? It's a wreck, a total and utter *disaster*.'

2

Caroline found it difficult to breathe; the estate agent's words flooded over her like she was drowning in them. 'Our employee who negotiated with your brother, was a crook.'

'A crook?' Caroline was sounding like a stuck record but it was the only way she could keep track of what she was being told.

The estate agent looked grim. 'He hoodwinked us all. He had been showing clients the wrong houses, forging photographs and papers, then pocketing the profits.'

Antonio's hand rested on the desk next to Caroline. It was as if he wanted to cover hers to stop it from shaking. The estate agent sighed. 'Your brother does now own a house called *La Casa di Spiaggia* and it is in a very desirable bay next to the sea. But instead of being the neat house in your photos, the real Casa has been empty for years and needs a great deal of work.'

Caroline stared at the photo of the decrepit house. There was nothing more to say.

★   ★   ★

Caroline and Antonio sat on the ferry heading for Sorrento. She was so numb she couldn't feel the swell of the waves. If it hadn't been for Antonio steering her through the crowds with a hand gently placed on the small of her back, she would probably still be sitting in the Estate Agent's office now.

They'd chosen the inside of the boat to escape the brisk breeze. Salt spray spattered at the window. 'I can't thank you enough.' She looked up at him as he handed her an espresso.

'It is a double, it will give you strength. You overestimate my input Caroline, I have done nothing of any use.'

'Oh, you have, just by being there. Poor Oscar, this will be such a blow for him after everything else.' Caroline went on to tell Antonio about him losing his wife and bringing up Izzy on his own.

'He sounds like a strong man, but being a Papa alone is very difficult. Girls need their Mamas, particularly teenagers. I have a sixteen-year-old sister, Louisa. She is a handful, wilful and headstrong. My parents despair of her. She is a dreamer with ideas of becoming an actress or model. It is true, she is incredibly pretty, but she is swayed by fashion magazines and the television. My father tries to make her focus on her studies but they clash constantly.'

With Antonio's easy manner, and captivated by his darkly sparkling eyes, Caroline felt a little easier. 'Izzy's never been a problem. I think she tries to look after Oscar as much as he looks after her. But I'm dreading breaking the bad news to them both.'

Caroline could see Antonio thinking as he put sugar into the tiny espresso cup and stirred slowly. 'Sometimes, a problem can be softened by offering up a solution at the same time.'

Taking the photos out of her bag and looking at them again, Caroline shook her head. 'But look at the beach house, Antonio. It's in a bad way, it needs rebuilding.'

'True, but listen; last year, we had an extension added to the hotel. The builders my father used were a small firm, but they did an excellent job and they have won many contracts on the back of that. I'm sure as a favour to me, they would look at the beach house and give you the fairest price for repairing it. That way, at least when you give your brother the bad news you can give him a way to fix it.'

'That would soften the blow.' As they were speaking, Caroline looked across the bay of Amalfi and saw a sliver of gold suffuse the grey ocean where the clouds were beginning to break and let the sun through. Looking at Antonio's concerned smile she couldn't help thinking that he was like that chink of sunshine. With his cheery face he would throw a bright light on any darkness. To come across someone like that was rare and she knew how lucky she was that he had been with her today.

As they parted at the quayside, the sun having finally chased away the drizzle, Antonio shook her hand warmly. 'I am sorry I cannot drive you back to the hotel. I have an appointment here in Sorrento with one of my father's suppliers, a local baker. I could cancel it and take you back.'

'No, please Antonio, I'm all right really. The hotel bus is so regular and I've troubled you enough today. But thank you.'

'Perhaps you would like me to contact the builder, Mr Ponti, and ask him to join us down at Paulo Bay tomorrow. He could look over the house and quote on what needs to be done.'

'That would be brilliant. As soon as I get back to the hotel I'm going to phone Oscar and ask him to come over on the first available flight. We could all meet you tomorrow morning.'

As he waved a cheery goodbye, and Caroline made her way up the hill past the smart shops selling lace and pottery, the impression of Antonio's handshake in hers made her tingle. She hadn't felt that since the day she'd met her ex-fiancé, Peter. But instantly, she checked herself and the spring in her step disappeared. Peter. Why did he continue to invade her thoughts? He too had seemed wonderful, he too had made her feel special and cared for. Until he showed his true colours, and those had only come out once she had agreed to marry him.

A shiver passed through Caroline even though the afternoon sun was now warming the tree-lined street. Deciding to break off her engagement with Peter had been traumatic. As she waited for the bus, she pondered all the lovers

42

hand in hand laughing and jostling their way into the town for afternoon coffee, and couldn't help thinking that what people showed on the surface was only part of the story. You could never understand a relationship until you were in it. She knew she'd had a lucky escape. Peter had seemed such a perfect fiancé, a professional man well-respected by his colleagues and friends; everybody told her what a perfect match he was, but only she knew the real truth.

Caroline's thoughts turned to Antonio. Younger, jollier than her ex-fiancé, he seemed so genuine, so uncomplicated, so unlike Peter. But how could you tell until you really knew a man? Antonio might also turn out to be a Jekyll and Hyde character. As she sat on the bus winding up the hillside with views of pastel-coloured houses and the Bay of Naples, Caroline resolved she must not allow herself to be attracted to Antonio. It was too soon. She could not go through all the ups and downs of another relationship, but must devote herself to Izzy and Oscar who had been there for her in the difficult times. That was settled, then, she told herself with a sigh. The very last thing she needed right now was a boyfriend.

★ ★ ★

When Caroline reached the hotel, she still had the task of breaking to Izzy that the dream holiday home was more of a nightmare. Her steps were slow as she went to the rooms upstairs. A knock on Izzy and Mel's door brought silence; they weren't at the pool either. Caroline went to reception. 'Have you seen my two companions?'

'Yes, they have gone out and left their key,' the lady on reception nodded. 'I remember because your niece was very excited, she said something about going down to the beach at Paulo Bay.'

Oh no. Caroline broke out in a cold sweat. Izzy must have persuaded Mel to take her down to the Casa. Caroline shot out of the door, over the road, and hurried down the snaking hill towards the beach. As she reached the end of the road with the picturesque bay spread out before her, she saw Mel and Izzy wandering by the beach, from one house to another. When Izzy caught her eye, she waved and ran over. 'Sorry, Auntie Caro, I was too excited to stay in the hotel. I persuaded Mel to bring me down here to wait for you. Isn't the sea gorgeous? Which one is our house, have you got the key?'

'Yes.' Caroline gulped. This surely was the worst moment of her life. Izzy's eyes were bright with expectation, her face glowing with excitement. If only Caroline could make it right, wave a magic wand so that Izzy's dream would come true the way Oscar had planned.

'We went into Sorrento and we chose Daddy's birthday present. It's a huge plant pot like the ones you see in the pictures of Pompeii. We thought he could put a bay tree in it and put it outside the front door of the Casa as a sort of welcoming tree. He'll love it. And we saw the most beautiful material for curtains, it was bright yellow with little red flowers — '

'Izzy.' Caroline despaired as she saw Izzy's eyes sparkling with expectation. She couldn't take this any more.

'See, I've brought down my music box; do you remember, Auntie Caro, the one shaped like a rocking-chair that plays 'Love me Tender'? It's the one my mother used to sing to when she put me to bed as a child. I brought it over specially from England because I want it to be the first thing that goes in the Casa. I miss her so much, but having it here feels like she's with us a little bit, even if she can't be with us properly. Do you think she's looking at us now from wherever she is? She'd be just as excited. Which house is ours?'

Caroline wished the earth would swallow her up. Her hands were sweating and a ball of anxiety knotted her stomach, making her feel sick. Mel and Izzy peered to where Caroline pointed. '*That* is the Casa.'

Izzy's smile had been as broad as the day but instantly it died on her face. She looked stunned, her eyes widening in disbelief. 'That one?' Her broken words were so quiet they could barely be heard. The only sounds were the waves rustling the pebbles on the shore, a bird singing from the tattered roof, the squeak of a broken shutter dangling in the breeze.

Mel gasped. 'No, Caroline, surely there must be some mistake; that place is rubbish, it's collapsing into the sea. Izzy, are you okay?'

The colour leached from Izzy's face. Her eyes darted from the crumbling roof to the tatty garden. Her forehead crinkled in dismay.

'Oh Izzy, I'm so sorry,' began Caroline, explaining quickly what she had learnt in Naples. At her words, Izzy's eyes pooled with unspilt tears. She looked dazed, and suddenly the hand which had held the music box tightly opened, letting the box crash onto the stones.

In a moment Izzy had fled. Away from the Casa. Down the beach, her hair flailing behind her. Mel knelt down to pick up the broken music box and Caroline set off after Izzy. The bay was only tiny. Once Izzy had run past the couple of cafes, past the small hotel and around the corner near the boatyard, there was nowhere else to go.

Caroline caught up with her at the small grassed picnic area. Izzy had flung herself to the ground, her body heaving with sobs. Caroline knelt down, grasped her in her arms and hugged as hard as she could. 'There, there, don't worry, we'll sort things, it'll all be okay.' Just holding the teenager's fragile body all skin and bone filled Caro's heart until she thought it would crack in two.

'But it isn't, is it? It just isn't, Auntie Caro.' Izzy's eyes were red and swollen, and tears splashed off her chin. Anger blazed in her words. 'That's exactly what everyone said when Mummy was ill. 'She'll be fine', 'she'll get better', 'she's a fighter'. Even Daddy told me, 'It'll all be okay', and it wasn't, it wasn't okay, it was horrible and the worst happened. People say they can fix things but they can't. Oh, Auntie Caro, I'm not just crying for myself, I'm crying for Daddy, he wanted this place to be so nice. He works too hard, he needs to rest, I worry about him sooooo much.'

Caroline lifted Izzy's face up and brushed salt-damp hair out of her eyes. 'Izzy, what a pair you are. Don't you see, Daddy wanted this place for *you*, to make everything somehow come right, even though we can't always solve things. He worries about you too. And he loves you very much.'

Izzy's wails had subsided into sobs. Caroline took a tissue from her sleeve and wiped the girl's swollen face and let her blow her nose. Gradually, when her breathing had eased, like a storm subsiding, Caroline said, 'Do you know the good thing about today?'

Izzy's bottom lip trembled as she

picked a tuft of grass and tossed it aside. 'There's nothing good about today.'

'Yes, there is, sweetheart. The good thing is that this is the first time I've seen you cry. Really cry and let it all come out. We've been so worried that you've been bottling things up, it's not good to do that you know. Crying's normal. You don't always have to be strong for your Dad, he'll get by.'

'Will he? I . . . I sometimes wish he'd find someone else. But that sounds an awful thing to say, I feel so guilty even thinking it. I don't want him to forget Mum, but I . . . '

'But you want him to be happy again. I understand. He won't forget her, and neither will you. She'll always be special even if someone else comes along. They won't replace her, they'll just be an extra person for him to care about. This is the first time we've talked about things properly, isn't it?'

Izzy paused and raised reddened eyes to her aunt. 'Maybe. Yeah, I guess it is.'

'Don't bottle things up, love, I'll always be here for you. Never forget that.'

Izzy grabbed Caroline in a bear hug. As Caroline held her, the sun beating down on them both, she felt for Izzy, and she also felt for Oscar. Surely being a parent must be the most difficult job in the world. With children you hold their happiness in your hands. Soon Izzy whispered in Caro's ear, 'Thank you.' And Caroline knew that somehow, some way, they would get over things. As long as they had each other.

★   ★   ★

Oscar arrived the very next day, an early-morning flight getting him to the hotel after breakfast. 'Okay, show me the way Caroline, you're the expert around here.' They set off for the ten-minute walk to the beach, Izzy sticking close beside her father, concern etched on her features. 'Well,' pronounced Oscar as they passed blue ipomoea vines and breathed in jasmine, 'the casa may not be all we'd hoped but this area is gorgeous. I've never seen so many wildflowers and the lemon grove is superb. You say it ends at the bottom of the casa's garden?'

'That's right,' answered Caroline, 'and you can buy the produce from the farm house: lemons, herbs, olive oil.'

'It's idyllic.' Oscar squeezed Izzy's hand and gave her a reassuring smile. As they rounded the bend, there was Antonio in deep conversation with Senor Ponti, the builder. The second he saw Caroline, he waved enthusiastically, causing her to blush and look aside. Hadn't she only yesterday made the decision not to contemplate another relationship too soon? Even though just seeing him caused a swimmy feeling in the pit of her stomach.

As Senor Ponti talked and they walked around the dilapidated cottage, Oscar nodded and Antonio helped with the translations.

'You know something,' Oscar said

after he and the builder had shaken hands and Senor Ponti had got into his truck and trundled off, 'I think we'll find a way around this. I'm just sorry to have to land more on you, Caroline, than I'd planned. Thanks to you, Antonio, I think Senor Ponti's offered me a very good price. Besides,' he looked over the bay at the sapphire sea, to the quaint bar with its tables on the sand and out to Capri shimmering in the distance, 'this has got to be one of the prettiest unspoilt places I've ever seen. We were lucky to get any property here. Also, I have some good news. They've made me a partner at work so I'll have a little more available to spend on the casa. It'll still be our dream hideaway.'

Caroline saw him watching Izzy's reaction and noted how the tense way he had been holding his shoulders dropped as soon as his daughter's smile returned. He shook Antonio's hand. 'Antonio, I've been delighted to meet you and I'm very grateful for your help.

Perhaps we could invite you to lunch or to dinner?' The regret was plain in Antonio's expression as he looked at Caroline and said, 'I really wish I could. Sadly, I am booked in to travel to a wine supplier and I shan't be back until late tonight.' So they said goodbye to Antonio and went off to make the most of the two short days Oscar had in Italy before having to get back home.

* * *

That evening before dinner, Oscar was having a nap, while Izzy was on the computer Facebooking her friends back in England.

'Why don't we go down to the bar and try some of that local limoncello liquer?'

Caroline was grateful to Mel for making the suggestion. She needed a distraction to take her mind off the day's events.

The hotel foyer housed a couple of shops which they hadn't yet explored, a gift and postcard shop, a jeweller's and a dress shop at which Caroline lingered. 'I could do with a new pair of sandals and these ones with the diamante flowers are lovely.'

'Nice, but expensive,' said Mel.

The owner of the shop, an elegant slim woman with perfectly painted apricot nails, wandered over. 'They are a bit more expensive than ordinary ones, but you can remove the diamantes and they come with other clip-on decorations, see — there are stars and daisies and these little pink roses. So in effect you get four different sandals for the price of one. I have lots of other designs at my other shop in Sorrento.'

As they were looking, they heard giggling at the back of the shop. Caroline turned to see the sullen waitress from that morning, Sophia, obviously off-duty with her hair up and teetering on high heels, chatting animatedly to a young girl who would have been a year or two older than Izzy. The younger girl, who had large almond eyes and a mane of curls tumbling down her back, was admiring herself in the mirror.

'Isn't she gorgeous,' whispered Mel, 'but I think that dress is a bit grown-up for her. Besides it's very tight.'

'I've tried to tell her,' the owner of the shop looked concerned as the girl disappeared with her friend back into the changing-rooms, 'it's too low-cut and much too short, but she won't listen. I know her father Salvatore, the owner of the hotel, and he'd hate it. What's more, I'll get into trouble for selling it to her. I've managed to get her to take some other more suitable outfits in to try on. But Louisa knows her own mind. What's more,' she said, frowning at Sophia, the waitress, 'she's easily swayed by others.'

This Louisa, thought Caroline, must be Antonio's sister. She remembered him saying she had ideas of becoming a model or an actress even though she was still only sixteen. She was certainly beautiful enough. Louisa reappeared again a moment later, and this time she wore an eye-catching turquoise jacket and trouser combination. The colour was perfect against her dark hair; she looked grown-up and elegant. 'No,' said Sophia with a grimace, 'it's just not you. I don't like it. It's the sort of thing my mother would wear.'

The proprietor moved over to try and counter Sophia's scorn. 'That suits you so much better, Louisa. The other outfit was . . . ' She hesitated as if struggling to find the right word.

'Trashy,' Mel whispered to Caroline.

'The other outfit was too much, I really don't think it did you any favours.'

'I liked it.' Louisa spoke perfect English with an attractive Italian lilt. Her words were clipped as if she were compelled to dig her heels in when faced with authority. Caroline guessed that she had reached that difficult age. Nevertheless, she hesitated while Sophia and the proprietor stood on either side of her like deer ready to lock horns.

Suddenly, a voice piped up behind them: 'If you don't mind my saying, the suit's really cool, much nicer than the dress.' Izzy had come down to find them. 'You look gorgeous in it. See here.' She flicked open a copy of the Elle magazine which had been tucked in her shoulder-bag. With its glossy pages showcasing handbags by Gucci and watches by Rolex, she loved to look at the photos and dreamed one day of being a photographer for them. 'There, that suit looks identical to this Yves Saint Laurent suit Kate Moss is wearing.' Louisa tilted her head to glance at the magazine; then, becoming properly interested as Izzy handed it to her, her pout turned gradually to a smile. 'Kate Moss, I love her, she is my favourite model. Do you really think I could look like her?'

'Absolutely, you've got the same high cheekbones. You see how she rolls up the jacket sleeves to soften the look and wears it with a classic white shirt, man's tie and impossibly high heels. You'd look ace. I don't want to be mean about that dress, but I've seen loads of copies of it in London, heaps of girls are wearing ones just like it, but they all look the same and it looks a bit naff now, it's very last season.'

'Naff?' Louisa looked perplexed. 'What is naff?'

'A bit O.T.T., you know, over the top.'

'Ah, I do not wish to look 'over the top'. That does not sound good. Maybe the suit might be better.'

'Absolutely, it would look great anywhere. Sorry to butt in, just saying.' With that, Izzy started to admire the sandals Mel was holding.

Louisa seemed to look at herself differently, then rolled up the sleeves and pondered, while Sophia had a face as sour as a squashed lemon. The proprietor seized the advantage and said: 'Here, Louisa, this crisp white shirt would give you the total look. I could even give you a discount if you bought the whole outfit together. What do you think?'

'At least I wouldn't get into trouble with Papa, I think he will like this outfit. And if it is what the girls are wearing in London . . . ' She looked towards Izzy who smiled encouragement. 'Yes, I will take it.'

When Louisa had left, with Sophia shooting them a look as they went, Caroline said to Izzy, 'Well done. You were so right.'

The proprietor looked relieved. 'Thank you for persuading her.'

'I was only saying what I thought.'

'It was your honesty that won over in the end. That Sophia is full of airs and graces, she's a bad influence on Louisa. Please let me introduce myself, my name is Kate Weston. You've helped me with my most important customer; the shop in the hotel is key for me because it encourages guests to go to my main shop in Sorrento. Please visit it while you are here,' she gave them all business cards from a silver case, 'and I'd be more than happy to let you have any outfit you choose at cost price. Anyone who helps me to keep the Salvatore and his daughter sweet deserves a reward.'

Caro bought the sandals and the three of them wandered happily off to the bar to wait for Oscar. Dinner was fun, with Oscar regaling them with tales of difficult clients and fusty old judges while Izzy excitedly told him she was to get a new, special outfit. Oscar looked intrigued. 'I must meet this Mrs Weston and thank her.'

'You can come when we go into Sorrento tomorrow and we'll show you the best ice cream shop in the world.'

After dinner both Oscar and Caroline were tired and went straight to bed. But Mel and Izzy were drawn outside by the warm evening. Wandering where their steps took them, they strolled up the hill, away from the hotel, towards the stars.

'You're quiet Izzy. Penny for them.'

'I was just thinking how pretty that

girl Louisa was. There's a group of pretty girls at school, but they just laugh at us geeks.'

'Nonsense, you're pretty and you're not a geek.'

'I wish I was more like Louisa, she's the sort all the boys go for.'

'Ah, some boys, Izzy, but not all. Beauty really is only skin-deep, and just because you don't wear lots of makeup or wear your dresses too short doesn't mean to say you aren't beautiful.'

'Maybe.' She didn't sound convinced. 'Next to someone like her, I look like a caterpillar beside a butterfly.'

'That's not true. Let me tell you something about when I was a teenager. I was a real tomboy, always in jeans, preferring to climb trees than sit and read. There was this boy all the girls swooned over, tall, silent and good-looking; they were desperate to go out with him. But guess who he chose.'

'You?'

'Yes, because I was different. He loved his motorbike and he was into sailing. He said all the other girls worried so much about their hair and their makeup he couldn't relax with them. I nearly fell over when he asked me out, and the other girls could hardly believe it. It just goes to show you never know what's around the corner.'

As Mel said this, they rounded a bend in the road and then halted in their tracks. Izzy gasped. 'Wow, what on earth are those? My god, it's like fairyland.' For there under the moon-light in front of them were a hundred twinkling lights dancing on the warm air from the hedgerow, rising and falling like grains of sparkle dust.

'What on earth are they? They're like sequins sparkling on a dress.' Izzy's big eyes opened wider at the spectacle.

'They must be fireflies. I've read about them but never seen them.'

'They're the most beautiful thing in the world.' Izzy scrabbled in her shoulder bag, took out her camera and started snapping. 'My GCSE photogra-phy teacher says we must always carry our cameras and never miss an opportunity. She'll go crazy when she sees these. They're so special. Wow, Mel,' she showed her the image on her digital camera, 'they've come out beautifully.'

'That's a superb shot. Let's catch one of the fireflies and see them close up.' She managed to cup one in her hands.

'Why, they're just ordinary old beetles when you catch them.'

'Amazing isn't it, how fantastic nature is.' Mel let the firefly go. They stood and watched the tiny creatures some more before setting back to the hotel.

Izzy looked up at Mel. 'You never told me what happened to biker boy, after he asked you out.'

Mel walked up the steps of the hotel and sighed. 'He asked me to marry him.'

'Oh, my goodness. I didn't know you'd been married.'

'I haven't. I turned him down.'

'Why? When he was so lovely?'

'He was. But you know, Izzy, sometimes you have to follow your dreams, because if you don't you end up like that firefly. If you feel captured your light goes out. I was thinking that only today when I saw Louisa trying on her clothes. She's a girl who wants to be admired and she's clearly rebelling against having her wings clipped. I didn't want to marry at the time, I wanted to work with children and travel, and I did, for a whole five years before I settled to looking after you. I was a nanny with a family who travelled to Switzerland, Malaysia, Africa, China, all over. It was fantastic and I wouldn't have missed it for the world.'

'And then you settled with us.'

'And then I settled with you.'

'Would you ever get married, Mel? You'd be a super mother.'

'No one else has ever asked me; but like I said, you never know what's around the corner. Besides, it's been an absolute joy seeing you turn from a baby into a child, and now nearly a young woman. Come on, let's get ourselves up to bed, it's been a long day.'

★　★　★

After Antonio pulled his car into the car park he rushed out, but just missed Mel and Izzy who had caught the lift to go upstairs. It had been a long day negotiating with the wine grower and he had been sad at having to turn down Oscar's invitation. Once again he'd had to put the needs of the Girasole above his own desires. All the while he had been talking about the price of bottles of white Lacryma Christi and red Taurasi Riserva, his mind had been elsewhere. It had been instead on blonde hair which curled in the rain, and beautiful skin, pale from a London winter, warmed pink by the Italian sun. There was something about the pretty young Englishwoman that stirred his blood and invaded his thoughts.

As he walked into the foyer, he heard

his father's voice. Salvatore rarely went to bed until the last guests had left the bar. As soon as he saw the older man, Antonio knew there was something up. His father's face which could as easily smile at a joke as bellow at an errant member of staff, looked at him sternly. 'It seems I have done nothing all day but answer the phone for you.'

'Why?' Antonio felt accused; he'd been out all day working for the good of the hotel, but it sometimes seemed, however hard he worked, his very presence could tip his father into a bad mood.

Salvatore tossed a piece of paper with a phone number towards Antonio. 'Your Professore has been trying to get hold of you. He wouldn't tell me what it was about. It seems he does not trust your father with information. He wants you to ring him instantly, whenever you get back.'

Antonio's heart leaped into his throat. Could this finally be the news he had been waiting for for months?

3

'Professore.'

'Antonio, my boy,' the Professore's voice boomed down the phone. Late though the hour was he was as ebullient as ever. Most likely full of a grand supper with friends and half a dozen glasses of the finest Vesuvio Rosso. 'Good to hear from you.'

Antonio's throat tightened. He had been on tenterhooks for months to hear whether the Professore had managed to secure funds for a major dig at Pompeii; and, more to the point, whether the committee had given Antonio the honour of being the student chosen to help with it. 'I have news.'

Antonio finally found his vocal cords. 'You do?'

'Yes, and there is good news and not so good news.'

Antonio twisted the phone cord in

his fingers; he wanted to hear the words but wasn't sure he could bear them. He wished his father would not pace outside the office like that. He always checked reception before turning in; but also, Salvatore must suspect that something was afoot, even though Antonio had kept as much from his father as possible.

'The good news is it looks as if I have secured the funds to carry out the dig. It is not quite in the bag but I am hopeful, very hopeful, my boy.'

'That's wonderful, fantastic news Professore. And the bad news?' Antonio felt his breath become shallow in his lungs. Bad news could only mean that one of the other students had been chosen, that Antonio had been dropped in favour of someone brighter, more intellectual and more available. Drat this darned hotel that kept him out all day discussing fripperies about wine and the price of bread, when the secrets of the ancient world yearned to be discovered on his doorstep.

'You have been shortlisted, you are now one of two candidates.'

Antonio leaned his hand on his forehead, struggling to understand. This, he had not expected. 'I don't understand, what does that mean?'

'The committee could not make a decision. Up until recently you were the only candidate in the running. But they were forced to consider the nomination of another candidate. I think you may have met one of my Tuesday students, Rick McPartlin, an American from New York. His father is a financier, richer than Croesus. That, I'm afraid, is where the funding is coming from. I have to say, young McPartlin is an accomplished classicist.'

There was silence whilst Antonio digested the dire implications of this and heard the Professore slurp another swig of wine.

'Didn't he study archaeology at Yale?' Antonio could feel his hopes deflating like a pinpricked balloon.

How could he compete with someone so well-connected and who was in such a marvellous position to oil the wheels of a placement with his family's money? He watched a moth that had drifted in, attracted by the light, and now flew round and round in the table lamp. Like that moth, he would be forever trapped at the Girasole, doing his father's bidding. 'So, that's it, then.' Antonio's voice was flat. 'I don't stand a chance.'

The Professore guffawed and Antonio wished his teacher hadn't imbibed quite so much wine. 'For an exceptional student you can at times be naïve, Antonio. If you want things in life you must fight for them, tooth and nail. Do you think I got to sit in this exalted seat without battling off marauders? People think academia is gentle and sweet but it involves as much political manoeuvring as the Caesars carried out in ancient Rome. The Archaeology Committee could show Berlusconi a thing or two about posturing. The next step, my boy, is that you and young McPartlin have been booked to come before the Committee with proposals: a worked-up plan for the dig now we know what funding might be available, showing how the money will be spent to best advantage. You can do that, can't you?'

'Of course, Professore, I did a business plan for the Girasole only last year. But seriously, looking at who is funding the dig, what chance do I stand?'

The Professore became stern. 'As much chance as the next brilliant student, my boy, never forget that.' The line went dead and Antonio was left holding the handset in silence.

'So, what does your Professore have to say that is so important?' Salvatore strolled into the office.

Antonio yearned to share his news with someone. If only he could talk to his father . . . but he couldn't possibly reveal how much he wanted to leave the Girasole. He cupped the fluttering moth in his hand and freed it carefully before locking the window. 'Just some stuff about university funding.' How could his father understand? But as Antonio stood to make his way up to bed, Salvatore reached out and laid a hand on Antonio's troubled shoulder. A tiny move of support. He patted his son, almost as if he were a little boy again. For a non-tactile man it was a mighty effort. Antonio yearned to hug Salvatore, who rarely showed affection, to thank him for his silent gesture and tell him everything. But in a second the moment was gone and so was his father, leaving Antonio at sea with his emotions like a lonely lighthouse in a raging storm.

* * *

'For your birthday, I think you should have the biggest and the best ice cream in all Sorrento.' Izzy pointed to the sundaes and multi-flavoured delights. 'How about that one, the tri . . . trico

. . . Well, the orange, white and green one in the tall glass with the flag and the sparklers in.'

'The *tricolore*, you mean.' Oscar chuckled, sure that it was the sparklers that she was most taken with. 'Do you know why that's the biggest and best? Because it represents the *tricolore*, Italy's flag. Let me see, pistachio, lemon and fragola — strawberry. With meringue chunks and sprinkles. What more could you ask for?'

'Chocolate. That's what. I'm going to have the *cioccolato misto supremo*, vanilla with choco chunks and hot fudge sauce all topped off with a profiterole.' Izzy rolled her eyes to heaven. 'How about you, Auntie Caro?'

'I've never had a *granita*, but that crushed ice with mandarin syrup will be lovely with an iced coffee.' Sitting at tables sporting white cloths that hurt their eyes in the morning sunshine, Izzy, Oscar and Caro spooned the rich, sweet concoctions into their mouths and watched Sorrento's main square.

Carriages drawn by horses, their tails plaited with crimson ribbons, trundled by. There was much meeting and greeting, kissing of cheeks and admiring of purchases as the locals went about their business, criss-crossing with tourists. For one moment, Caroline thought she'd spotted Antonio in the crowd. But it wasn't him, and she realised that although yesterday she had tried to keep her distance, his easy smile was never far from her mind.

'Shall we just sit here and eat ice cream and drink espressos all morning?' Oscar stretched his legs and put his hands behind his head. Caroline could see him unwinding by the minute. She'd felt guilty about contacting him but this mini-break seemed to be doing him good. If only he could stay longer.

'No, daddy.' Izzy, who'd gone off taking photos of the horses, grabbed his hand to pull him up. 'We promised to meet Mel at Mrs Weston's shop. I don't know if she'll have anything I'd like, but she said my reward for smoothing things with Louisa would be to choose something at cost price, whatever that is. You never know, she might do men's stuff too. Italian men look soooo cool; you could look that cool too Dad, you're not *that* old, you know.'

'Oh, thanks for that vote of confidence. Now, where on earth did I leave my walking stick?' Oscar joked as they set off, with Izzy careering on ahead so she could window-shop.

'She could do with new jeans,' Caroline remarked, 'she's got a growth spurt on and those ones are far too short.'

'You know I can't tell bootleg jeans from a pair of flares. Shopping's about as much fun as root canal work at the dentist in my humble opinion. But as long as they've got a chair I can plant myself in and read the newspaper, I'll cope.'

Mel was already flicking through a rail of summer dresses when they arrived. 'These are just gorgeous, Kate has such nice stuff here.'

Caroline watched Oscar stifle a yawn and make for a sofa in the corner when Kate Weston emerged from a back office, a cloud of Chanel No. 19 in her wake. Only a gently curvaceous figure and limbs tanned the colour of biscotti could have carried off a peach-coloured shift dress with such aplomb. An elegant updo and tiny pearl drop earrings were understated and as fresh as a fruit sorbet. As Kate greeted Izzy with, 'I'm so happy you found my shop, come and see what I've got,' Caroline turned to haul Oscar out of his chair and away from the lure of the newspaper.

But he was already at their side, his hand outstretched, his jacket smoothed down and the paper forgotten. 'So you are Kate Weston; I've been hearing all about your business. Izzy here is desperate for some new jeans. I see you've got loads in stock. Perhaps you could show us what would suit her best. We might even need two pairs, um ... in different colours or something.'

Izzy looked as if she'd just heard her father speak in Martian and Caroline shot Mel an amused glance as Oscar earnestly started discussing the merits of Levi's over white skinnies, his eyes all the while not on the jeans at all, but on Kate Weston's pretty face. 'Well,' Caroline whizzed over to the rail where Mel stood pretending to keep her attention on the sundresses, 'I thought Oscar had got to the stage where the only thing that excited him was a new brief from his lawyer's clerk, but perhaps I was wrong.'

'I think you were very wrong,' giggled Mel. 'Perhaps it's something to do with all this sun. Or perhaps it's just that Oscar appreciates an elegant, feminine woman when he sees one rather than those ultra-serious lawyers with their sensible shoes and mousy hair he's tried dating. Whatever, I think that Izzy may well end up with quite a few bags of pretty clothes, don't you?'

* ★ ★

Caroline looked out for Antonio at dinner and afterwards wandered into the garden which had been transformed by his carefully-planted jasmines and new tangerine bougainvillaeas. She'd found herself trying extra hard with her appearance this evening and had worn a dress she hadn't been able to resist from Kate Weston's shop, pure white cotton with pintuck detailing; it was cute and summery. She kept telling herself that she only wanted to see Antonio because Oscar was keen to connect with him before returning to England, but in reality he'd invaded her thoughts all day.

As she peered from the garden terrace overlooking the sea, in the distance she saw Louisa sitting on the wall by the quiet road. Suddenly the silence was broken by a scooter, buzzing its way up the hill like a wasp. She wasn't at all surprised to see the young man riding it screech to a halt next to Louisa and jump off. '*Ciao bellissima.*' He puffed out his chest as she tossed her curls in his direction. Caroline was studying the two of them in deep conversation when she caught a tang of lemony aftershave and fresh shampoo drifting to her on the still evening air.

'Uh-oh, my father isn't going to be pleased about that.'

Caroline's heart did a backflip at Antonio's deep tones as he came to watch his sister. Something about him today made him look weary, his eyes had lost their sparkle. Caroline tried not to sound delighted that he'd caught up with her and said nonchalantly, 'Surely Louisa's allowed to speak to boys her own age.'

'Some, yes. The ones who go to very good schools and will go off to college and make something of themselves. But that boy rides his scooter round these roads like he has a death wish. What's more, my father saw him hanging around in Sorrento smoking cigarettes on a day when he should have been in school. My father has warned Louisa to keep away from him.'

At that moment, a bellowing sound made them jump as they saw Salvatore come out on the steps gesticulating. 'Louisa, Louisa,' he boomed. She jumped off the wall and her lip pouted. Sharp words were exchanged while the boy backed off, skulking away before he climbed back on his motorbike and burnt rubber into the road as he disappeared.

'What's wrong, has she done something very bad?' asked Caroline.

'It depends how you look on it.' Antonio's expression was pained, as if he was listening to breaking glass. 'She says she is doing nothing, and in fact she was telling that boy to go away and stop bothering her. My father, on the contrary, says she must have been encouraging him to make him pull in to speak to her. Now she is hurt, saying he never trusts her, and that when our mama is away like she is now, he keeps an even tighter hold on her so bad she feels she is suffocating. If I don't go down and see them, blood may be spilt.'

'Of course, only . . . '

'Only what?'

'Oscar had been wondering if you'd like to join us in the bar; he wants to buy you a drink for referring us to your builder, Mr Ponti.'

Now Antonio looked much more animated, less weary. 'I'd love to. I will sort out my father and sister and will see you in there. Promise you'll wait for me.'

'Of course.' Caroline was flattered at his keenness and, as she watched him disappear then emerge outside moments later, speaking in soft tones and pouring oil on troubled water, she could see how much both Salvatore and Louisa relied on him to help glue them together. He was a born peacemaker. Every member in a family has a role, and Antonio's was clear. Salvatore must be keen to keep his son close, not just to run Girasole, but because he was the hub around which young and old united.

A moment later, back in the bar, Antonio came in, his arm around his sister. She seemed placated but sullen until Izzy, keen to show everyone her new Italian clothes, bowled up. 'Louisa, would you like to come and see what I got today at Kate Weston's shop? Please tell me what you think. They're in my room. Have you worn your suit yet? I got a fantastic blouse that would look great with it, although I don't think we're the same size, what size are you . . . ?'

Izzy's chatter faded into the distance as they went up in the lift together leaving the adults in the bar. Over the cheering bubbles of a bottle of Asti Spumante, Oscar explained how he had paid a visit to the Chief of Police to discuss the scam that had led him to buying the Casa. 'I am determined the perpetrator will be bought to justice. Interestingly, I've just started working on a case of internet fraud back in London.'

'It must be difficult for the police to keep up with IT criminals, they can be very clever,' said Mel.

'One of the things the fraudster did was to construct an internet site almost identical to the estate agent's, that, as their website was opened, would super-impose itself in front of the real site, giving false information. Like hanging an extra picture over the original in a frame. It's very difficult to detect but they have assured me they are working to catch the perpetrator and have some good leads. I was concerned that I still had a legal title to the property so I can go ahead and fix it, and thankfully I have.'

When conversation turned to Antonio, it became apparent why he had been under a cloud earlier as he explained the position with the Professore. 'It sounds to me,' said Oscar sagely, 'as if the Professore has a tough job on his hands. Money is so difficult to get for purely research purposes.'

'If the worst came to the worst,' sighed Antonio, 'I would prefer that the funding still comes in to my university to do the work, even if I have to give up hope of helping with the dig and let the American help instead.'

'But that's terrible.' Caroline found herself defending Antonio. 'You've been wanting this for ages.'

'Since I was a tiny boy and went to Pompeii with my parents. You must pay a visit while you are here,' he addressed them all.

Oscar shook his head. 'I have to leave shortly as I have work in London, but I hope to be back next weekend. Kate Weston told me of a touring opera group that I'm very keen to see. But you should visit Pompeii soon, Caroline. It would be better to go at this time of year before it gets too hot.'

'I could take you tomorrow, it is my day off.' Antonio sat on the edge of his seat. The ruins had been top of Caroline's list of things to see, and although she didn't want to encourage Antonio when she had resolved not to even think of boyfriends at the moment, it would be a fantastic opportunity to tour the legendary antiquities with an expert.

'My flight leaves early in the morning, Caroline. But you could take Mel and Izzy.'

'Yes, come with us, Mel.'

'I'm afraid it would bore me to tears. Besides, Kate's offered that Izzy can go and help in the shop tomorrow, with the chance of taking loads of fashion shots for her GCSE portfolio. I'd set my heart on going round the food shops.'

So it was arranged that just Caroline and Antonio would go, and despite herself, Caroline felt butterflies swirling in her stomach as Antonio shook her hand when he bade them goodnight.

★ ★ ★

Antonio couldn't sleep. Even reading the stodgiest of tomes on life in Roman times couldn't chase away wakefulness. So, he'd wandered up the hill, to the far end of the Girasole's land above the hotel. Sorrento twinkled below a star-filled sky, the night air smelt of sweet earth. He sat on the log he'd always sat on as a boy when he played under Salvatore's watchful eye, his father picking up the dust and sprinkling it into his fingers, saying, 'This is your land, be proud of it.'

When Antonio suddenly heard wheezing and the crumbling of stones he thought it was some snuffling animal making its way along the fence between the Girasole and the neighbouring land of the Casiraghi family. 'Papa,' he cried, reaching out to help his father. 'What are you doing up here at three in the morning?'

'I might well ask you the same, my son, you scared the wits out of me. I thought it was that old goat Casiraghi.'

'Papa. Don't tell me you are fighting again.'

'Not at the moment, but we will be, before long.'

'Papa, you've been scrapping since you were teenagers at school. Isn't it time you grew up?'

'Hah, it is not me, it is him. Look at what the underhand son of a no-good snake in the grass has been up to.' Salvatore took a torch out of his pocket and shone it near the fence posts. 'See, when we weren't looking, the old fool has dug up the fence posts, moved them to steal a little bit of our precious land, and covered the holes over again, thinking I am too feeble-brained to notice.'

'Surely he wouldn't do a thing like that.'

'Wouldn't he?' But clearly the earth had been moved. Antonio knew this part of the garden like the back of his hand. Salvatore was right, a subtle half a metre had disappeared. 'He's been looking to buy the Girasole for years, but I'll never sell. This is your legacy. He's resented me ever since your mother chose me over him when we were youths. If only your mother were here now, she would talk some sense into your sister. But, I'm glad she is away looking after your grandmother; if she were here to see this she would fret and end up even more ill than your poor nana.'

'Papa, don't get angry, it's bad for you.'

'Antonio,' Salvatore's eyes narrowed, 'I've battled many things in my life. I thank the Lord you are here to help me protect the Girasole. Your sister and her nonsense over that boy and those ridiculous clothes she wears are just the latest of my troubles. But I've never given in and I won't now. Tomorrow we go out to buy concrete to set those posts in. If it kills me, Casiraghi's not going to get his greasy fat fingers on any more of our land.'

* * *

Izzy, Mel and Caroline sat with their feet up on Caroline's balcony devouring fresh fruit for lunch. Below them was the verandah leading out from the dining room. Mel suddenly put down the nectarine she was quartering and frowned. 'Look, isn't that Sophia, Louisa's waitress friend? She's looking a bit queasy, do you think she's okay?'

Izzy got up to look. 'So it's true then.'

'What is?' asked Caro.

'I shouldn't really say anything, because Louisa told me to keep it a secret, but Sophia's pregnant. She was in tears the other day.'

'Why?' Mel looked concerned. 'Doesn't she want a baby?'

'Oh yes, she does, very much. But her husband's just been made redundant from the local factory. She's terrified Antonio's dad will give her the sack once she can't wait on tables any more.'

'Oh, I'm sure he wouldn't do that.' Caroline regarded Sophia who, after taking gulps of fresh air, appeared to rally and went back into the dining room.

'Well,' Izzy started to clear up the plates and throw away the peelings,

'Sophia's not so sure. It's all come at the worst time for her, she and her husband had just bought a small boat off a friend and they still haven't finished paying for it. She said none of that would carry any weight with Salvatore. She reckons Antonio's dad is a hard man and all he thinks of is business.'

Caroline shared a look with Mel. 'Well, don't believe everything Sophia tells you, Izzy, she's inclined to see things entirely from her own view. And Louisa's not too happy with her father at the moment. I'm sure those two girls have a fine old time grumbling about Salvatore together, but it's not easy running a big hotel and being head of a family when your wife's away. Come on,' Caroline continued, 'it's not good to gossip. Let's get our things together and have a game of Scrabble by the pool. You won the last one, Izzy, now it's time to give me and Mel a chance to get our own back.'

★　★　★

'Here it is.' Antonio stretched out his arms. 'Pompeii, the most wonderful archaeological site in the whole of Italy. Perhaps the world.'

'It's breathtaking. I'd never imagined it would be so huge, I sort of forgot it was a whole city. These roads are like a maze. I'm so glad I came with you, I'd have got lost just with Mel. And it's so wonderful to be able to come here after hours when all the tourists have left. There's a real atmosphere in the quietness, especially with Vesuvius towering above us.'

'It is one of the privileges of working with the Professore, all the security men know me. As long as I ring beforehand I am allowed in after hours. Do you not feel we are like time travellers here, Caroline? See, you can put your feet in the ruts along this road, and feel where the wheels of ancient carriages have worn the giant cobble stones.'

The city was gradually coming alive for her as he pointed out frescoes and the faded stones of mosaics which had been placed by fingers of men alive in 79AD. She thought back to Peter, her ex-fiancé. He had been pleasant to spend time with but very intense, often liking to do things together in stillness and silence like listen to classical music. Sometimes it had been like spending time with a statue, the two of them reading together in opposite chairs. Watching Antonio bound through the streets she felt his liveliness, his vibrance. He delighted in showing her new things, in communicating with her and hearing her views. She was full of questions. 'What are these L-shaped stones for?'

'They are the counters of little bars and restaurants where the proprietor would stand, calling at people to come in for a bite to eat during their working day. I often imagine the noise in these narrow streets, the cries of shopkeepers, the clanging of hammers on anvils from the blacksmiths, the barking of dogs, the sprinkling of the public fountain by the old well where travellers would fill their leather canteens with water on a hot day. Rich and poor lived side by side.' They strolled on and Caroline found herself captivated by his tales of discoveries. 'Here is the House of the Triclinium, where diners lolled on couches eating figs and apricots with egg and honey custard. We discovered food remains during the excavation of the House of the Vestals. Seeds and bones, painstakingly sifted to remove centuries of dust, have each told us a little more.'

They travelled to and from Pompeii by train as Antonio said it was the easiest way to go; and, as they strolled back through the warm evening, they lingered, as if neither of them wanted to come back to the present. 'Would you like to see the old harbour?'

'That sounds lovely.'

They wound their way down through the streets to the harbour with its lights dancing on the water. An ivory moon rose, reflecting like silver coins on the sea.

'I cannot remember when I enjoyed an afternoon so much.' Antonio turned to her. He was close; she could see the bronze tints in his hair and the flecks of amber in his deep brown eyes. As he held her in his gaze, she felt special, admired. 'I never realised English girls were so beautiful until I met you.'

Caroline shook her head; she just didn't believe it. She considered herself very ordinary, pale and uninteresting, next to the fulsome Italian girls with their wide mouths and long eyelashes.

'Please do not shake your head.' Antonio took his hand and placed it gently under her chin. As she felt the soft pressure of his finger stroking her jawline, it was as if time had stood still; as if the moment had been suspended, like the moon reflected in the gently lapping waves. The evening was sublime. He leant closer; she caught her breath, she ought to pull away, no way should she allow him to kiss her; but she couldn't move, her heart pattered inside her chest, until suddenly . . .

'Antonio, *buona sera, ciao.*' A group of young men and girls rounded the corner and swept them up in boisterous chattering and laughter as Antonio, with a wistful look in his eye, acknowledged their slaps on the back and introduced her to his friends.

When they finally got back to the hotel, the magic had faded and the real world had crashed in. The moon had slipped behind clouds. As if he didn't quite know what to say, Antonio wished her a gentlemanly *'Buona notte,'* making a slight bow, as he left Caroline to make her way upstairs, still wondering what it would have been like to be held in his arms.

★　★　★

'I miss Oscar already.' Caroline and Mel had taken a walk through the gardens while Izzy Facebooked her friends. 'He looked so relaxed here. But at least he's coming back on Friday for a long weekend.'

'To check on Mr Ponti's building work?'

'That's what he said, but more I guess to take Kate Weston to the open-air opera.'

Mel looked concerned. 'Isn't she married, though? She is after all Mrs Weston.'

'Separated, apparently.'

'That sounds a bit complicated.'

'Mmm. But we're all a bit complicated, aren't we, we all have history that makes us wary of starting new relationships.'

As they wandered back through reception, Caroline was passed a note. 'It's from Antonio. He says, *The forecast today is unseasonally hot with sun before storms later. Do you all fancy going down to Paulo Bay after lunch? I can show Izzy the best place to swim, and we can see how Mr Ponti's doing on La Casa's roof.*'

'Sounds great,' said Mel, 'although I don't know if I'll be swimming; it looked a bit rocky. But I can read my book, and if this afternoon's as muggy as it was yesterday, a sea breeze would be great.' They left a message taking up the offer, fetched Izzy and wandered down to the beach fully equipped with towels.

It felt easier being with Antonio now they weren't alone. '*Ciao*, Signor Ponti.' Antonio chatted with the builder about the roof. 'He says all the tiles have had to come off and he has new ones coming tomorrow to make the building watertight. It looks clear now, but a storm is due this evening, so he will rig up a plastic cover to protect the interior. We can come back to check tomorrow.'

'Thank you Antonio. They seem to be working really hard.'

'Can we swim now, I'm so hot.' Izzy was red-faced. 'I'm desperate to try out my underwater camera.'

'I will show you the best place on the beach.' Antonio led the way. 'Here by the bar is only good for paddling and leisure swimming. It is sandy but too shallow for much sea life. Over there,' he pointed to a rocky outcrop, 'that is best for viewing fish and creatures such as sea urchins. If you jump off that big rock it is like swimming in an aquarium.'

They set up camp on the rocks at the edge of the bay which jutted out into the sea providing a natural jetty. 'There are little bays like this all along the coast. Are you coming swimming too, Caroline?' said Antonio as he took off his top, ready to jump in in his cut-off jeans. All the swimming and gardening had given him powerful shoulders, a flat stomach and a well-defined nut-brown torso which reminded Caroline of the athletes on the Pompeiian frescoes.

'Absolutely!' The water refreshed them in an instant, and it was amazing to see silver fish dart near their toes.

'Watch me dive under, Auntie Caro, there are some wonderful fish deep down, and they're so tame and easy to catch on camera.'

When she came up, Antonio admired

her photos on the little digital window. 'The *polpo* looks fantastic, although I prefer mine on a plate fried in butter with lemon.'

'Uuurgh, you mean people eat them?'

'Octopus can be delicious, Izzy.' Mel had looked up from her book and come over to see the photos.

'No way could I eat something with eight legs and suckers.' Izzy screwed up her face.

The afternoon seemed to get hotter as cloud cover came over and shut in the heat. They idly explored the rock pools, Antonio patiently naming all the creatures for Izzy in Italian, until the sky began to turn grey. 'A storm is definitely brewing,' Antonio said, his hair spiky with sea salt. 'Maybe it is time to pack up.'

'Oh please, can I go in just one more time before we go? I want to try and catch a picture of that big fish, the one with the yellow stripe.'

'Okay, one more time.' Antonio looked for Caroline's nod of approval before he and Izzy jumped in. Caroline started to bag up the drinks they had brought. As she did so, she noticed in the distance a flash of lightning far out to sea, and a swell develop on the waves. Mel dozed, her book dropped by her side. Suddenly, Izzy screamed.

'What is it?' Caroline rushed to the edge of the rock.

'Don't worry,' called Antonio, 'it is just a shoal of *medusas*.'

'What? I don't understand!'

'Don't jump in, Caroline,' Antonio yelled over Izzy's frantic splashing, 'I've got her.'

Mel woke as Izzy started to shriek. 'Ow, ow, it hurts! Like I've been cut on my finger.'

'Here.' Antonio's voice was commanding as he swiftly grasped Izzy's arm and lifted her skinny body up onto the rock. As he hoisted her to safety, the last thing Caroline saw was Antonio yell in pain and sink below the surface, disappearing into the sky-blackened waves as another crack of lightning stabbed the sky.

'Where's Antonio?' Izzy cried out while Mel draped a towel over her and studied the tiny red welt on her hand. 'What happened, what on earth are *medusas*?'

'Oh no, that's what stung you.' Caroline pointed into the water and there, floating in the choppy waves, menacing tentacles drifting behind them, was a massive shoal of jellyfish. Caroline gasped, suddenly realising how much she had come to like Antonio and how scared she was that he was nowhere in sight. The sea had swallowed him up and thunder roared overhead.

4

Caroline didn't know which way to turn, where to run. 'Antonio, Antonio,' she yelled at the top of her voice. Her hair whipped across her face in the squally breeze.

'Auntie Caro, I can't see him anywhere.' Tears welled up in Izzy's eyes. She swept them away with the back of her hand. 'Antonio, please come back?' Fat blobs of rain spattered onto the rocks.

'He'll be fine.' Caroline struggled to hide an inner scream, her voice breaking as she clutched Izzy's shoulders to still the youngster's shaking body.

'I'll go and get help.' Mel scrambled off the rocks whilst Caroline and Izzy scanned the choppy waters, desperate for a sight of the brave young man who had hauled Izzy to safety before thinking of himself.

'What if . . . ?' Izzy bit her lip, unable to speak.

He's gone for good. The words jumped into Caroline's head. She fought to push them out as she stood, ready to leap in and help Antonio. The choppy grey sea, like an angry monster, licked at her feet. She had to be strong — for Izzy. Desperate to convince them both, she said, '*Nothing's* going to happen to him. He's young and strong. He's been swimming off these rocks since he was a boy.'

On edge, Caroline nearly slipped off the rocks herself as she whirled around at the sound of a motor launch bouncing across the waves. Mel, wrapped in a waterproof, stood next to the pilot, pointing to where they'd last spotted Antonio.

Caroline's spirits leapt. 'Look, Izzy, someone's come to help. They'll find him. As soon as you see any sign of him, point him out and they'll pick him up.'

The minutes ticked on. Behind her, Caroline was conscious of a wailing ambulance screeching to a halt on the sand. The launch scanned the length of the beach, then returned and circled where Antonio had disappeared. The pilot looked up at Caroline, raised his hands in a Neapolitan gesture of despair, and shook his head. Thank heaven Izzy was looking the other way and didn't see. Another boat, white with a red stripe, hove into view on the horizon. The Italian coastguard.

'Oh, over there.' Izzy's voice raised an octave as she squealed and pointed frantically at something bobbing on the waves a good hundred metres out from the shore. The launch and the coastguard boat zeroed in on it. Caroline's heart lurched; please God they had found him. The coastguard boat approached, put a long pole out into the water, and lifted ... an old battered sack, dripping and lifeless. Antonio was nowhere to be seen. A low growl of thunder agitated the waves and the wind blew keen and brisk.

⋆   ⋆   ⋆

'Blessed Madonna save me, save me.' Antonio's thoughts screamed in his brain as his lungs felt fit to burst and spasms of air bubbled out of his mouth. He had been swimming underwater too long. He must surface now but the menacing cloud of jellyfish blocked the way above. 'Madonna, Madonna . . . ' His lips formed the words frantically as his mouth filled with salt water. To distract from the agony he knew would come when he swam through the jellyfish, he pictured the beautiful face which used to look down on him in church. But there was no avoiding it. He soared upwards to the surface; tentacles brushed against him, and pain like the sting of a thousand angry bees scored his back. He yelled, finally breaking the surface of the water. Where was he, where was the beach, where was Caroline? Sweet, kind, enchanting Caroline. 'Please God, let me see her again.' Rocks loomed up, unfamiliar, jagged. With the last iota of strength left to Antonio he dragged his aching limbs through the waves. 'Must . . . get out.' He hauled himself onto the slippery shore and staggered to a stand, only to have his legs crumple under him. Immediately, *thwack* — his head hit the rocks. A massive jolt of pain went through him. Then, there was no more pain. No more fear. Just empty, black, oblivion.

* * *

The ambulance men threw waterproofs over Izzy and Caroline, having per-suaded them, in stumbling English, to come onto the beach where a cluster of locals had gathered. Loud Italian voices made Caroline dizzy. When a hand was placed on her arm, she turned to find a middle-aged woman holding out a cup of coffee, steaming

107

in the thunder-charged air. She was handsome — rich chestnut hair framing her face. It was a good face, with a kind smile, a strong no-nonsense nose and classic full Italian lips. Beside her a boy held out a glass of warm milk to Izzy, dark eyes radiating concern. His gangly limbs reminded Caroline of Labrador puppies before they grow into their oversized feet.

'Offer the ladies some *panettone*, Rafaele. *Mangiare, mangiare*, eat, eat; it is good for you, even in times like this.' She urged the boy forward. Caroline took some to be polite, but the cake with plump sultanas and bitter coffee was so comforting she realised how long it was since food had last passed her lips.

'You're very kind, you shouldn't have.'

Izzy smiled weakly and nibbled a mouthful while Rafaele's mother looked on appreciatively.

'Nonsense. All these energetic coast-guards are doing everything possible to find your friend, but those left behind need care and attention too. Rafaele and I, we are your neighbours.'

'You are?' Caroline liked the way the woman rolled her Rs when she said *Rafaele*. When Caroline saw Izzy turn down a second slice of *panettone*, she noted the relieved look on Rafaele's face. Now the guests had eaten their fill, he was allowed, after a nod from his mama, to finish off the slice; which he did, in seconds.

'Boys, always eating. Especially at fourteen years old, they are as hungry as wolves. Yes, we are your neighbours. We own the lemon grove and the olive trees next to the old fisherman's cottage. It is our house where you can buy the olive oil. It is good to see La Casa being fixed finally. I thought it would be swept off into the sea, it has been so neglected. It was once a happy home. Rafaele's nana who lives with us has old photographs of when it was thriving.'

'It is my brother who's bought La

Casa and I'm here with a friend, Mel, she's out in that boat helping to look for Antonio.' Caroline looked anxiously out to sea.

'The young man, Antonio, will be found soon. Try not to worry.' Rafaele's mama was being brave for all of them.

Caroline managed a weak smile. Her new friend was working so hard to buoy them up. 'Mama's right,' Rafaele chimed in, all the while looking at Izzy's troubled wide eyes. 'We have stood here many days waiting for news of boats and people who have gone astray. The waters here are kind, not vicious. The currents are not cruel.'

The brief moment of relief from worrying about Antonio allowed Izzy's hurt finger to trouble her again; she licked and blew on it.

'But you have been stung.' Rafaele peered at the red welts on Izzy's finger. 'You must not let that put you off swimming, it is possible to avoid them. They float in clouds so you can dive underneath them and resurface when it is clear. Come with me, the ambulances carry antiseptic cream which takes the pain away.'

'Your son's lovely.' Caroline handed back her empty cup to Rafaele's mother. 'And you both speak such good English.'

'Rafaele's father was English.'

'Ah.' Caroline didn't know what else to say, as the other woman clammed up, holding her chin high. The father was obviously no longer around. The silence hung heavy. There was so little they could do whilst all the frantic searching was going on. 'Well, thank you for your kindness. My name is Caroline.'

'And mine is Beatrice.' She said it the Italian way with the C pronounced like the *ch* in church. 'Has anyone informed the family of the young man who is lost, what has happened to him?'

'Oh no.' Caroline felt guilty. 'I didn't bring my mobile phone to the beach.'

'Then hurry and use our phone; it is just a few minutes' walk to our house,

111

you can be back very soon. Rafaele will look after Izzy.'

★　★　★

Immediately Caroline entered Beatrice's old farmhouse, she felt some small measure of relief. The kitchen was the hub of the home. From a pot on the old-fashioned range delicious smells of bubbling chicken, garlic and oregano filled the air. French windows looked out onto the lemon grove, the olive trees and the sea. From the ceiling was suspended a bleached wooden dryer dangled with pillowcases. A dresser of cheerful blue and white plates took up one wall. The scrubbed pine table held a dozen chairs, and over them were suspended what looked like long ribbons covered in flour. 'Oh,' Caroline exclaimed; it was such a bizarre sight, it quite took her back.

'We are drying *tagliatelle*.' Beatrice placed a loving arm around an older lady who stood by the cooker in a jet-black dress and flat shoes, her cloud of silver hair bobbed under her ears, her hands covered in flour. She was short and round, with a small silver crucifix at her neck.

'Rafaele's Nana makes her own pasta.' The older lady bobbed her head in welcome, beckoning Caroline to a seat. But Beatrice gabbled a stream of Italian as she hastened with Caroline to the telephone. 'I have told Nana you must get back.'

Caroline phoned the Girasole whilst Beatrice and Nana looked on, exchanging worried glances. Caroline explained everything to Antonio's father, who said he would come immediately.

'I wish I could stay, but I must go back.'

'Of course,' said Beatrice. 'We understand. Have faith, my friend. The young man *will* be found. Come back and visit your neighbours very soon when things are better for you.'

Caroline looked wistfully at the domestic scene: so safe, so normal. It had been only a few minutes, but the break from the dreadful situation, and Beatrice's strength, had stilled her heartbeat, restored her spirits and enabled her to run back to the beach with new hope.

★ ★ ★

Salvatore's eyes were hooded as he arrived on the beach. Worry lines spider-webbed from his eyes. He stood with his arm around Louisa, but it looked more as if she were holding him up. The powerful man appeared to shrink under the strain. For once, Louisa was not dressed to the nines but was scrubbed of makeup, her luxuriant hair scrunched back in her hurry. Caroline went over to them, her heart stabbing at the concern in their eyes.

'I'm so sorry. There's no news yet.'

Salvatore's chin was firmly set. He rested a hand on Caroline's shoulder. 'Thank you, for letting us know that my son was missing. He's very important to us.'

'He's important to me too.' The words blurted out before Caroline had a chance to stop them.

'I know.' Salvatore managed a wise smile. 'My son has talked about you many times. I have noticed his English improving by the day.'

A strawberry blush ran up Caroline's cheeks. She'd never spoken to Antonio's father, he always looked so gruff, but she could see how much his son meant to him. Antonio had told Caroline of his father's recent problems with their neighbour Signor Casiraghi, who had tried to steal their land, and Caroline could see the man's shoulders rounding under the weight of all these troubles. 'I hope I shall be able to teach him some more, not that he needs it. Antonio is so clever.'

'He will be head of the di Labatis one day. In Italy we talk about *la famiglia*, the family. A good family is as energetic as a football team, as strong as a mountain and as important as the air we breathe.'

'Don't worry, Papa.' Caroline had seldom seen Louisa so caring. When the chips were down, the teenager loved her stern father with a passion. 'Let us get out of this dreadful rain; we can see the sea from the coffee bar, we will know immediately if there is any news.'

Reluctantly, Salvatore agreed, nodding his head and succumbing to a hug from the coffee bar owner who greeted his old friend from up on the hill. Caroline and Izzy walked up the beach to the far end by the modern boatyard with Rafaele. He knew a path that would take them up the steep road above the beach.

'From there we can get a good view of the whole bay and beyond. My Nana used to come up with me when she was younger, and point out the shoals of fishes clouding the sea. It is an old fisherman's trick. When my Nonno was alive the two of them would go up there to decide which way he should take the boat out. He would say it was necessary to walk towards heaven if you wanted to see the bottom of the ocean.'

As they made their way up, Caroline could feel hope waning, her eyes clouding with the teeming rain. They stood in desperation. It was an hour and a half since Antonio went missing, but the boy was right. From this distance, inlets along the coast which were not visible from the beach could be viewed from the hills. Then, Rafaele squinted his keen eyes. 'Look, look over there, by the cave. Something is moving.'

'What cave?' Caroline peered to where he pointed. By a large gaping black hole, far around the rocks she could just make out what may, or may not, be an arm, emerging from underneath a lump of seaweed. When a lightning flash illuminated the sky, she was sure. The three of them dashed down the hill, around the boatyard, waving and shouting to the coastguard.

Antonio heard a noise. Waking was like coming out of a long dark tunnel, like emerging from a pit. As he turned his head, he saw through the squall the shore coastguard's launch chugging into view. His prayers had been answered. His spirit sailed up like a rocket.

They had to help him walk, but as they wrapped him in a blanket, he felt the life coming back to his body. As the boat hit the shore, he desperately scanned the people. Only one person mattered. There was only one pretty, dear face that he yearned to see. He climbed out of the boat, rain pouring off his face, and stumbled to her. This time there was no hesitation, no stilted politeness, no holding back as he grasped Caroline's face in his hands. The raindrops tumbled off his sodden hair, but her smile was the only thing that mattered. The rest of the world was at a distance. The cheers from those waiting came to him like a dream, for all he could feel was the warmth of Caroline's cheeks in his hands, the closeness of her body trembling against his, and finally, as he brought his lips down on hers, their softness.

Joy poured through his veins like warm liqueur as she sank into his kiss and warmed him with her slender limbs. Her blonde curls dripped down her back. He no longer felt the chill of the rain, for everything was all right. The whole world which had stood still was now turning as it should do. Because she had searched for him. She had found him. And given herself up to him in front of the watching world.

*   *   *

'They're going to keep him in for a couple of hours for observation, but he's fine.' Relief had spread across Caroline's face, serene as the blue sky which had replaced the storm. Mel had met her from the hotel bus and they were coming through the Girasole's entrance. 'Salvatore and Louisa are waiting for him at the hospital. I would have stayed but I felt he needed time with his family.'

'Those jellyfish stings looked awfully red, and all over his back and legs. Poor Antonio.' Mel winced.

'They were horrid. He told me he normally knows exactly what to do when a shoal comes near the shore; they are common here, and usually he just swims underwater and surfaces in a clear patch of water. But the storm brought in twice as many as usual, he couldn't find a break in the shoal and was gasping for air, so he had to swim through them. Thrashing about, swimming for his life and disorientated by the rain, he got further from Paulo Bay until, exhausted, he staggered into the cave then passed out. It must have been terrifying. Salvatore was beside himself. He really is a very caring father, and he was so sweet saying we'd helped to save his son's life.'

'And they're letting him out later on?'

'Yes, he'll be back this evening.'

As Mel and Caroline collected their keys from reception, they were conscious of raised voices over where the plush shops were by the lifts. Caroline started to walk faster. 'Isn't that Kate Weston and the hotel manager arguing? And who's that other man in the blue suit? They seem to be giving her a hard time. Come on, she looks as if she could do with a hand.'

'I haven't miscounted. The money is definitely missing.' Kate's normally unruffled air was fraying at the edges.

The man in the blue suit was leaning in towards her, speaking in a loud whisper through gritted teeth. 'There is no way a member of my coach party would steal from you. This is the first day of their tour and they're awash with holiday money. I wish I'd never showed them your shop. I've given you good business, now you're turning around and accusing us of stealing.'

'Is everything okay?' asked Caroline, conscious that the guide in the blue suit had invaded Kate Weston's personal space and was jabbing the air with his finger.

'All I know, Mr Sage, is that your first coach party came into my shop en masse in the morning, and it's true lots of them bought things. Then I closed for lunch and the afternoon was briefly quieter until you bought the second coach party in and it was chaos again. But when I cashed the till to close up, there were five hundred euros missing. I can only assume it was a member of your tour who stole it. We'll have to call the police.' She turned to the hotel manager who held his head in his hands.

'Can this not wait for Mr di Labati, the hotel owner, to return?'

'I am not having my people accused of stealing on the first day of their holiday.' The tour guide was getting louder by the second.

'But they will be gone in a couple of

days,' Kate pleaded, 'and if nothing's done I may never see that money again.'

Caroline felt sorry for the poor hotel manager who looked despairingly at the two of them. He had to keep both these people sweet, so it was hardly surprising he was in a state of paralysis. If Salvatore had been here, he would have been strong and made an instant decision, however difficult it was. Caroline knew the importance of the brief summer season to Kate's takings, and that the Girasole's reputation would be a top priority for Salvatore. They could not have money disappearing and nothing being done.

'Well, I'm going to call the police if no one else is,' she announced and, leaving Mel to comfort Kate Weston, made straight for the phone.

Within twenty minutes, a polished policeman in plain clothes and his assistant had arrived. The Inspector wore a crisp Italian suit, a white shirt and had a shaved head which gave him an air of hardness, although his bright blue eyes betrayed inner softness, particularly whenever he happened to glance over at Mel — which he did probably more times than was necessary for the purposes of his investigation. Having listened intently to everyone's story he said, with a lilting Italian accent, 'Well, we do not want to accuse anyone unjustly. So before rushing to get statements from the members of your tour party, Signor Sage, I would like to choose another angle of investigation.' He turned to the hotel manager. 'I see you have a CCTV camera in reception. Does it record this area?'

'Yes, *Commissario*, most certainly; the whole of the reception is included, it is the busiest place in the hotel.'

'Good. Give me the films for the times in question and set a room aside. Perhaps, Mrs Weston, you would come with me to study them. And,' here he made a polite little bow and glanced yet again at Mel, 'if you would like your friends to come and support you, that would be useful.'

It was one of the few times Caroline had seen Mel blush, but she had to admit the inspector was strikingly good-looking in a hard-man way. The three women accompanied the Inspector and the hotel manager ordered coffee for them, pleased that the unpleasant scene was moving away from the glare of the public.

★　★　★

A celebration lunch to mark Antonio's recovery took place the next day at Beatrice's house in the midst of the lemon grove. 'It's very kind of your mother to invite us all, are you sure she can cater for that many people at short notice?'

Rafaele welcomed them in. 'Of course. Nana and Mama love a full house. My Nana was so excited to get out all the special plates and cutlery, she has been polishing and dusting like a crazy woman.' Rafaele busied round,

hanging up jackets, enquiring after
Antonio's good health in swift Italian,
shaking the hand of Oscar who had
returned for the weekend, compliment-
ing Mel on her attempt to pronounce
buongiorno and saying in an aside to
Izzy, 'I have made something special for
you, I will show you after lunch.'

The dining room looking out on the
lemon grove had been made up with
white cloths and gleaming cutlery. The
sound of the waves could be heard in
the distance. But instead of showing the
guests in there, Rafaele lead them
straight to the kitchen. The scent of
thyme, bay leaf and rosemary hit their
noses and Nana, a smile beaming
across her face, passed them all an
apron. At their polite but quizzical
looks, Beatrice explained. 'You said you
might like to try your hands at making
pasta and it takes only minutes. We have
done all the sauces and grated the
cheese so, if you would like to have a
go . . . '

'Sounds like fun,' said Mel, tying the

apron behind her back. Caroline broke eggs into flour, stirred and kneaded. Izzy turned the wheel on the pasta machine, while Mel dusted the kitchen table with flour. They giggled at Oscar's lumpy pasta dough which, under the kind tutelage of Nana, magically turned into strips of smooth tagliatelle. And they marvelled as Beatrice taught them to roll ravioli dough so thin you could see the knots of the wooden table beneath. 'Only that way,' she explained as they helped Nana to fashion round blobs of ricotta and spinach and press them into pasta parcels, 'will your ravioli be perfect.'

Caroline was beaming. 'I never thought making pasta could be such fun. Antonio, perhaps the guests at the hotel might like to spend a day learning to cook in a traditional kitchen? It would make a change from going on coach tours.'

'And they could buy freshly-pressed olive oil and bottles of limoncello from Beatrice to take back as souvenirs. It's a good idea, Caroline, we will mention it to my father.'

Sauces of cream, tomato with basil and rich truffle were spooned over their steaming homemade pasta as they collapsed to eat at the dining room table. Pinot grigio and rich red chianti flowed. Caroline and Mel recounted to everyone the theft at Kate Weston's shop and there was much speculation as to what might have happened. 'Such things are always difficult,' said Beatrice, 'no one wants to make a fuss and spoil anybody's holiday. But such wrongdoing mustn't go unpunished.'

Finally, after a dessert of tiramisu, different members of the party peeled off to enjoy the leisurely afternoon. 'Please,' Beatrice opened the French doors wider, 'enjoy the lemon grove, or have some more coffee at the table as you wish — *la mia casa è la sua casa* — my house is your house. Nana and I are going to wash up and Rafaele and Izzy have offered to help.'

'Nonsense, you must let us help.'

Oscar got up but was ushered firmly back into his seat again to enjoy coffee and Baci hazelnut chocolates with Mel, whilst Antonio and Caroline filtered outside into the sunshine.

'What a perfect lunch,' Caroline said as she and Antonio wandered down towards the sea and stood at the boundary between the lemon grove and the Casa di Spiaggi.

'It is only perfect because I spent it with you.' Antonio's hand sought out hers and held it. But Caroline could not turn to face him and her hand remained lifeless in his. She had known this moment would come and she'd been dreading it. The waves sparkled back and forth over the beautiful bay, the sun warmed her bare arms. She looked at the spot on the beach where Antonio had gathered her into his kiss. She had replayed that scene a thousand times during a sleepless night, and each time it had been intense pleasure . . . spiked with unbearable pain. Because she knew what she must say to him and it was going to tear her heart in two.

'Antonio.' Gently, she pulled her fingers out of his and forced her hands behind her back. 'Yesterday, what happened in the heat of the moment, it can't happen again.'

Antonio's smooth brow creased, his bright eyes dulled. 'Why? Caroline, *cara mia*, all the time I was out there, swimming, desperate to get back to shore, was because I needed to see you again. Because you have become the thing I think about night and day. I am never free of you.' He bit his lip, as if he was holding back words for fear he might declare too much. It left a small red mark that she longed to put her finger on, to smooth away the hurt.

'Antonio, you mustn't. Please. You're a wonderful person, so kind, so good, so clever. You need a wonderful woman who can return all that. But I'm not that woman. I've been burnt, Antonio, by a love affair that went very wrong. I . . . I was engaged, not long before I came out here, but everything fell apart.

I'm broken inside.'

'Then let me put you back together.'

'No Antonio, I'm so sorry, but it's not as simple as that. I'm not ready. I'd only disappoint you.' *Besides*, she thought, *one day I will have to leave this paradise and get back to work and back to my real life.*

'You could never disappoint me.'

'Please.' She held up her hand to stop him coming closer. 'I don't want to lose your friendship. Please say we can still be friends.'

The scented Italian breeze drifted through the lemon trees and nudged Antonio's fringe over his eye. If only, if only they were lovers, she could have leant out and brushed it back, felt the silkiness of his hair under her fingers, felt again the fullness of his lips against hers. But it wasn't to be. The silence hung heavy, the space between them seeming endless.

'Auntie Caro.' Izzy bounded out of the French windows and through the lemon grove clutching something in her hand. 'Look, look what Rafaele gave me, he made it. When I told him mine was broken, he gave me this one as a housewarming present to replace it.'

The young boy ran close behind her. Caroline reached out and Izzy placed in her hand a music box. In white wood with green leaves and a lemon inlaid on the surface, it was similar to the ones they had seen in all the shops, but this was a little rough around the edges, a little homemade, and all the better for it.

'I have been learning from my uncle who owns a workshop, how to make these boxes. This one was to be a Christmas present, but I can easily make another by then.' He lifted the lid for them and a pretty tune mingled with the sound of the waves.

'What's it playing?' asked Izzy.

'*Torna a Surriento*,' replied Rafaele.

'What does that mean?'

Antonio turned his deep soulful eyes towards Caroline. 'Come back to Sorrento.'

Izzy and Rafaele ran off to show the box to the others. Caroline bit her lip. 'Friends?' she asked.

Antonio nodded and his smile fought to hide the sadness in his eyes. 'Friends,' he said quietly. But they wandered back separately through the lemon grove, each deep in their own thoughts, and Caroline watched Antonio disappear into the house on his own.

Oscar strolled up and put his arm about his sister. 'Are you okay?'

'Yes, of course. I'm fine.'

'You know, Caroline, I often wonder if you did the right thing breaking off your engagement to Peter. Being alone doesn't suit you. I could never see why you split up.'

'Those things are always complicated, aren't they, but we just didn't have the same values. Peter was so extravagant, it frightened me. He'd book a table at the Dorchester or the Ritz at the drop of a hat when it wasn't even a special event. I'd have been just as happy with a home-cooked meal, and I don't think you can go through married life wasting money like that.'

'But Caroline, Peter's a financier, they earn a fortune. That sort of thing is a drop in the ocean to him. You know I still see him at the odd social event, don't you?'

'I assumed you might do.'

'He was asking about you the other day.'

Caroline didn't know what to say. She felt so confused. 'He was?'

'Yes. He still has feelings for you. When I see you looking sad, like you did just now, I wonder whether you two couldn't give it another go.'

'Please, Oscar. I . . . life isn't that simple. Your offer to come out here has given me a rest from all that, a rest I badly need.'

'Okay, Caroline. I was just thinking, that's all. You know me, I like to sort stuff.' Oscar breathed deep, as if he was thinking of a way to change the subject. He looked back from where they'd come. 'What a fantastic bay this is.' Then, Oscar's face formed into a frown. 'Surely it's not still siesta time is it? We've been here for hours and I haven't seen any workmen at La Casa. I came down for a quick stroll after breakfast and no one was here then either. Hmm, I think it's about time I got in touch with Signor Ponti and found out what the hell he's playing at.'

* * *

It was dusk by the time they all left Beatrice and walked back up the hill into the Girasole. Caroline tried to enter into conversation but she was painfully aware of the gulf she had created between herself and Antonio. It would have been so lovely to return his affection, and she was fonder of him than any man she had met since Peter, but for that reason she couldn't bare to think of anything ending badly. Not allowing something to begin felt safer. But what was the right thing to do?

Oscar had mentioned Peter, and Caroline realised he, too, often invaded her quiet moments.

It was, then, a welcome distraction when the hotel manager approached them as they were all saying goodnight by the lifts. 'Signorina Beaumont, the Commissario has been on the telephone. He has asked that you ladies meet him here, with Signora Weston, after breakfast tomorrow morning.' Caroline was sure she heard a sharp intake of breath from Mel at the mention of the inspector's name. 'He has been looking through the CCTV film and has spotted something of great interest. He thinks he might have seen the person who committed the theft.'

5

'Mel,' Izzy's eyes were wide, 'you're looking dolled up this morning. Going somewhere special?' Izzy held Oscar's hand and was dressed in shorts and yellow T-shirt for a morning down at the beach with Rafaele, while Oscar had arranged to have a discussion with Signor Ponti. Mel and Caroline sat in the lounge, sun pouring through the window, waiting for the Commissario of police.

'No,' Mel tried to look nonchalant, 'I just wanted to try my new skirt and top. When I get back to England it'll most likely be raining and that's not the weather for lilac linen.'

'But you've curled your hair. And you never wear eyeliner, it's great, you look very . . .'

'Young and pretty,' Oscar butted in, sensing Mel's embarrassment. 'Every-one makes an effort on holiday because they have more time. Come on, Izzy, I've got to have words with Signor Ponti today over the slow progress on La Casa, and I'm not looking forward to it. Thank goodness I have this evening's opera with Kate to enjoy.'

They left, and Caroline felt for Mel, who brushed non-existent dust from her skirt and didn't know whether to sit or stand. The Commissario was ten minutes late, which only increased Mel's agitation.

'Ladies.' He arrived, wafting essence of pine-forest aftershave into the hotel. He gave a bow from the waist, old fashioned but full of gentlemanly appeal. 'Please accept my sincerest apologies for having kept you. An incident with a large dog and an even larger lorry in the town kept me.'

'Oh no, I hope the dog wasn't hurt.'

'Don't worry.' When he spoke to Mel, Caroline noticed his voice soften and his smile widen. 'The dog escaped in the peak of health. The lorry unfortunately did not. I had to stop the driver inflicting as many wounds on the dog owner as the crash had inflicted on his lorry. Luckily, in true Italian fashion there was more shouting than actual blows. I was peacemaker. I would never normally be late for an appointment.'

'Of course we forgive you, Commisario Mazzotta,' Caroline said. 'We don't have anything else planned for today. You said you had some CCTV footage to show us.'

They went through to the office behind reception where Kate Weston joined them. They were beckoned to sit down by Antonio, fully recovered from his jellyfish stings and back at work. The Commissario ran the film, then stopped and pointed. 'The picture is grainy, like snow. But see here, this dumpy figure, in a raincoat and scarf. It is impossible to make out her face in those sunglasses, but she waits outside until your shop is very full, Mrs Weston. Then she goes in only when you are distracted with customers.' He wound the film on. 'There is something strange. She does not emerge, even when you close the shop for lunch.' He ran the film back again so they could all see. 'She never goes to the front of the shop, but keeps to the shadows. You were too busy to notice with all these people picking up stuff and asking prices. What is at the back of your shop?'

Kate thought for a moment. 'There's the stock room which is normally locked, and the changing rooms which were full that day. It was so busy. I was on my own. I remember I had to unlock the stockroom to get out various sizes.'

'Do you remember locking it?'

'No. Oh, it was so busy both before and after lunch, I can't remem . . . Oh, goodness. I do remember something. I wanted to lock it during the day but couldn't find the keys. I gave up searching and found them next day on the floor.'

'Let us look at later on.' He fast-forwarded the film. 'There, see.' A crowd of the coach party jostled with bags and umbrellas because of the rain. He rubbed his chin in deep concentration. 'There, she is emerging. Quickly, she is gone. That is your thief.'

Kate peered at the screen. 'She looks middle-aged the way she's stooping, and she's obviously overweight. Who is she?'

'That is why I am here today to see if any of you recognise her.' He raised a questioning eyebrow looking first at Antonio, then round to each of them. Kate said, with a note of despair, 'I have no idea. The only distinctive thing is that the belt of her raincoat is a replacement.' Kate pointed at the screen. 'See, the raincoat is light grey and the belt is dark; someone has obviously lost the original and grabbed a black one. Apart from that it's a mystery.'

'One thing is for sure.' The Commissario switched off the television. 'When you pulled the window blinds and went to lunch, she took the money and hid. Later she sneaked out and made her escape. She is our thief.'

Once they had seen the footage, the Commissario offered Kate and Mel a lift into Sorrento. He asked them to call him Cesare, and Mel had piped up with, 'That's such a lovely name.' Then she put her hand over her mouth as if she was afraid of speaking out loud what she was thinking.

Caroline smiled as she watched the three of them leave the hotel. She saw the Commissario put his hand gently on Mel's back to steer her away from an over-exuberant child. He could have charmed the oranges off the trees.

As for Caroline, she still felt bad about her conversation with Antonio at Beatrice's lunch party, when she had made it plain she just wanted to be friends, no more than that. She feared losing his friendship and he had appeared uneasy this morning. A move to patch things up was necessary.

She followed him out to the swimming pool where he fished for fallen red geranium petals with a net. 'Antonio, are you okay? You seem distracted. I hope it's not because of our chat.'

Antonio leant on the net. Caroline couldn't bear to see him unhappy. He was normally so bright and breezy and helpful to others. To think something she had done might have brought him down cut her like a knife. She longed to reach out and place a hand on his shoulder, but that wouldn't have been fair. Besides, he kept his distance.

'There is a lot going on with this theft. I wish my mother was here to help. Papa relies on me even more when she is away, but my grandmother is still unwell. My head is full of jobs which need doing around the hotel. But what I should really concentrate on is my presentation to the Archaeology Committee. It's my bid to join the important dig at Pompeii.'

'Yes, of course; that's today, isn't it?'

'This afternoon, after siesta time. I have gone over it, but I'm not used to public speaking and they are the most crusty old academics at the university. I have butterflies in my stomach. I shall open my mouth and have nothing come out. It's driving me crazy.'

'How would it be,' Caroline bit her lip; she desperately wanted to help, 'if we went somewhere quiet and you showed me your presentation? I'll give you honest comments, then hopefully you won't be so nervous when faced with a roomful of important people.'

'That's kind, Caroline, but I couldn't inflict it on you. It's a very dry presentation, all about costings, flow-charts and digging up old ruins.'

'Nonsense. I'm as fascinated with Pompeii as you are. Besides, that's what friends are for, to help each other out.'

He nodded. A half-smile told her she had achieved her objective. They were just platonic friends. Yet now she had that sorted, she really wasn't sure that a simple friendship was all she wanted with Antonio. Today he was looking entirely delectable in smart black trousers and shirt. His hair tousled, he could have been an Italian movie star. Life was so complicated.

* * *

'So Cesare dropped you in Sorrento. Then what happened?'

'Nothing,' Mel twirled round her bedroom, taking first one dress then another out of the wardrobe. Holding them up, she considered her reflection in the mirror.

'Nothing? Hmm. Is that why you're trying out *every* outfit you own? Come on, spill the beans.'

Mel grasped her hair, twirling it round her head, pinning it first in a sultry fashion over one eye, then trying a side parting. 'Well, maybe Cesare did take me for a coffee, just so he could tell me about his home town and interesting places to visit.'

'And . . . ? Come on, Mel, I know that walking-on-air feeling. What else?'

'Maybe he happened to mention he was free tonight, and might I fancy a trip in his open-topped sports car, for dinner in Amalfi?'

'Oh, that's wonderful, Mel, how exciting. Going out with a policeman.'

'Isn't it? What do you think, the green or the red?'

'The green, definitely, it's more demure and so, so pretty. I love that light chiffony material, especially for a warm evening. Goodness, there's you off for dinner, and Oscar off with Kate to see the opera.'

'And you all on your own.' Mel sat beside her on the bed.

'I'm fine,' Caroline protested. 'Izzy and I will wander into the town. I hear the Easter celebrations are on. People dress up in white cloaks and hoods and process silently down the street with lighted torches. It's meant to be very moving.'

'Caroline, Oscar's really worried about you. He thinks you're lonely without Peter. He's convinced you're missing him. He thinks you ought to patch things up. Now Oscar's all loved-up with Kate, he can't stop talking about her, and feels everyone should be in a couple.'

'My darling brother is sweet but he doesn't understand. Peter seemed perfect but he was controlling. I'm glad I broke off the engagement. Peter earns pots of money but he thinks that entitles him to be top dog, leader of the pack. Life with an alpha male wasn't for me. I know Oscar bumps into him in his work but he never sees that difficult side of Peter. Anyway, he's a man, he doesn't understand; I need a partner who'll let me be my own person. You look lovely in that dress. I'll do your hair later.'

When Caroline got back to her own room, she was surprised and touched to see a bunch of flowers left outside her room, pink roses and jasmine. On them was a card in flamboyant swirly handwriting. 'Thanks for your help. The presentation went well. I know the American student will win the place. But at least with your help, I put on a good show. Antonio x'. Poor Antonio; she gazed out of her window at the ocean in the distance, and felt sad for him to feel his dream slipping away.

★　★　★

The next day, Antonio felt better. He was sure he wasn't going to be chosen for the dig at Pompeii but was determined to be practical and had resigned himself to his fate. He bumped into Oscar coming out of the breakfast room.

'Hi, how did your presentation go yesterday?'

'I gave them my best. But they will choose Rick McPartlin. His father is donating funds for the dig. Rick's a nice guy, but his father's pushy. He owns a chain of stores back in the States and is the sort of guy who seals every deal personally. He flew over from California to schmooze the committee. They wined and dined him like a prince.'

148

'But that's unfair to you as the other candidate.'

'You English are so keen on fair play. Italians are more pragmatic. I wouldn't blame the committee for favouring Rick over myself, they need that funding. Where are all your girls?'

'Mel and Caroline are lingering over breakfast. Izzy's gone for a swim with your sister. She and Louisa'll be out sunning themselves by now. By the way, thank you for your help with Signor Ponti yesterday. He really got cracking after you'd had a word with him.'

'I was straightforward. I told him he wouldn't see any more work from The Girasole Hotel unless he finished your beach house soon. Plus we have some urgent fencing work at the back of the hotel and his men are doing that. That's them arriving now.'

'Good. I might pop up in a bit and have a word with the foreman, there's something I need to ask him.'

'Feel free.'

Antonio supervised the men as they

lugged concrete posts and bales of wire up the hill behind the Girasole's garden. That in itself, and mixing the concrete, was a morning's work. The fence was looking good now, fine and solid. 'Papa, you didn't need to come up.'

Salvatore had puffed up the hill and was getting his breath back. 'I do. I want to see the job done properly.'

When the work was nearly finished, Oscar appeared with Caroline. 'They're doing a very thorough job.' He took the opportunity to have a word with the foreman about the best colour for the Casa's paintwork. Suddenly, the air was shaken with a terrific bang. A gunshot ripped through the air. Caroline screamed and Antonio rushed to her side.

'What in heavens name was that?' Oscar said.

A stocky man with thick grey hair crashed through the undergrowth, a hunting rifle under his arm, pointing up to the sky. 'What do you think you're up to, di Labati? Get your filthy hands off my land, *cialtrone*!'

'*Your* land?' Salvatore puffed out his chest like a pigeon. 'Put that gun down, *vecchio perdente*. Come and fight like a man.'

'Papa, don't.' But Salvatore pushed Antonio away, squaring up to his opponent.

'*You*, Casiraghi, have been trying to steal *my* land. Just because Valentina chose me over you all those years ago. I saw what you did, moving my fence-posts. You, stinking rat, are a disgrace to the name Casiraghi.'

'Papa, you will say something you regret.' Antonio held his father firmly now.

'You could not fight your way out of a bowl of pasta,' Signor Casiraghi yelled, putting the gun on the ground behind him and rolling up his sleeves. 'Come on, *vecchio rimbambito*, come on.'

'Bah.' Salvatore panted with effort. 'You are not worth it, Casiraghi. What's more, I have a lawyer here to see the work is done correctly.'

Antonio saw Oscar turn pale, but then clear his throat and play the part. 'Well, yes, ahem; I am a lawyer. This all looks in order to me.'

Signor Casiraghi staggered back, defeated, humiliated, and pointed at Salvatore. 'You've dishonoured my family name. You will pay for that.' So saying, he picked up the gun and stomped off up the hill.

★   ★   ★

'Is your father okay?' Caroline was concerned that Salvatore was overwrought after his confrontation. Antonio was standing by reception holding a letter in his hand, his brows knitted into a frown.

'He will be alright, Caroline. Thank you for asking.'

'Not at all. I have a lot of respect for him. He's a good man in a difficult world.'

'That is true. He has been worrying about the theft from Kate Weston's shop. And there is another reason why he went off the rails. This letter is from Mama. She says my grandmother, Nana Bonetti, who has recently had an operation, has taken a turn for the worse.'

'Oh dear. Can't the doctors do anything about it?'

'They have given her pills for angina but Mama says there is something on her mind. I am very close to Nana Bonetti. She looked after me while my parents were working all hours building up this hotel. Mama has asked me to take a trip to see her. Nana Bonetti has a secret she cannot tell even the priest. If only Nana could get well then Mama could return here to help Papa. Her absence is getting him down. I must go.'

'Are they far away?'

'No. My grandmother only lives across the water. She retired to the Isle of Ischia. You can make it to Ischia and

back in a day. It is a beautiful place.'
Then Antonio suddenly perked up. 'I
do not like to ask favours, Caroline, I
know we are . . . like you said, only
friends.' Her heart ached as his chin
appeared stern and controlled but his
deep, dark eyes betrayed inner yearn-
ing.

'Ask away.'

'Well, I should like you to meet my
mother and my grandmother. Having a
visit from someone from London would
be fun for them. Bring the outside in.
Would you consider coming with me? I
can show you the most beautiful island
on this coast.'

'Of course,' Caroline agreed readily.
Her stomach flipped at the thought that
Antonio wanted her with him, even if
only as a friend. 'Oscar has told me he
was able to get this week off work to
spend time with Izzy and supervise the
builders at La Casa. I would love to see
Ischia. It sounds exotic.'

* * *

Caroline and Antonio took the early morning hydrofoil over to Ischia. The sea shimmered gold as a spun silk scarf drifting on the breeze. Shoals of fish darted like silver arrowheads as the ferry nosed through the water. 'It's breathtaking,' said Caroline filling her lungs with the cool salty air.

They stepped off the ferry into a taxi which wound them through narrow streets towards Nana Bonetti's house. 'It will not be long now.'

They flashed past shops with long strings of white garlic bulbs and curly red peppers suspended like little devils' horns hanging out to dry. Caroline sniffed Mediterranean herbs and spices on the breeze. Oregano, basil, and rosemary teased her senses. They stopped at a set of red lights where Caroline heard the noisy chatter of two ladies standing next to a stall selling oversized black grapes with a grey bloom and a sign saying *Uva*. Her Italian was improving by the day. Next to them was a box of large, greeny-red tomatoes, and lemons the size of grapefruits with sprigs of leaves still attached. Everything here grew bigger, more colourful than anything she had seen in England.

When they rounded the corner to where Nana Bonetti lived, Caroline was entranced. Nestling over a tranquil turquoise bay a jumble of houses hugged the hillside. They were painted in peach, lime, pistachio and cream. Offset by emerald hills, the houses' reflection shimmered in the water of the bay.

'That is our house, the pink one with the verandah looking out over the sea with the palm tree in the garden. It is tiny but cosy. Mama is at the window looking out for us.'

Antonio's mother Valentina hugged Caroline like a long-lost daughter. Nana Bonetti sat in a wicker chair on the verandah, looking frail but delighted to see the grandson who towered over her. '*Bambino, bambino,*' she cried as she kissed Antonio, and wiped the corners of her eyes with an embroidered hanky.

His mother beckoned Caroline aside to the kitchen. 'Perhaps you will help me make salad, we have beans and fresh tuna with garlic olive oil dressing. I am going to prepare a tomato and basil salad. We grow our own on the balcony. The tomatoes are still warm from the sun.'

'I'd love to.' She and Valentina chatted about cooking and varieties of fish Caroline had never heard of, such as garfish and bogues. In an hour, they had a table of cold dishes fit for a five-star restaurant. Slices of deep red salami took their place next to Parma ham. Artichokes in sunflower oil were sprinkled with black olives. When Valentina bid them all sit at the table on the verandah, Caroline felt the meal could not have been more perfect. The waves whispered in the background and Nana Bonetti squeezed Antonio's hand in between courses. The old lady laughed at Antonio's jokes, a little squeaky sound, as she joked with him, nudging him and nodding towards Caroline, her misty eyes mischievous and playful. But, Caroline noticed, she only picked at the delicious dessert of baked apricots with amaretto and creamy mascarpone cheese. Clearly there was something on her mind.

'Antonio, my child, it is wonderful of you to come and to bring such a pretty companion with you. My family are good to me but I am such a bad person.'

'Nana.' It was the first time Caroline had ever seen Antonio angry. 'I won't hear you say that. You have always inspired me. What on earth could make you say that?'

She looked down at the white table cloth and tugged her handkerchief until Caroline thought it might fall apart with all the wringing. 'Something happened many years ago now which I feel a dreadful guilt about. I have never told anyone, never.'

'Nana.' Antonio raised her chin to

look at him. 'You can tell us, whatever it is; surely it will help to share with those who love you.'

She took a deep breath. Her knuckles had turned white. 'You are right. This secret has plagued me, it has kept me awake at night and blights my old age. It is time to make amends.'

The air was heavy with silence.

'When I was a girl during the war, I fear I may have caused a man's death or imprisonment.' Caroline sat up sharply, paying more attention. Valentina blinked, her hand to her mouth.

'I was just eight years old and I was running an errand for my mother to an adjoining farm. The war was a misery for us. God forbid that you should ever know such appalling treatment. We were hungry every moment of every day, we lived in constant danger, occupied for years by Nazi bullies who terrorised our mothers and belittled our fathers. Their word was law. I was walking back over the fields when suddenly I heard a fighter plane in the distance. As it came nearer, I saw the red, white and blue circle on its wings and knew it was an English plane, but there was smoke pouring from its undercarriage. When I saw a pilot bail out and land I was terrified. So rooted to the spot was I that I literally couldn't move. The poor wretch of a man ran up to me, blood streaming from a horrific gash on his head. I wanted to run, I didn't understand. I nearly died of fright when he thrust a piece of paper with writing into my little basket. I screamed and I'll never forget the look of terror in his eyes as he stared around. Then I ran as fast as I could.

'Like a cowardly mouse, I did not help him, I did not tend his wounds or even grace him with a comforting smile. That poor, poor man. He would have had a wife back home, children who loved him, he was injured and I . . . I just deserted him.'

She buried her face in her hands, but she did not cry. She held in her misery and looked up first to Valentina, then

Antonio, who had placed a firm hand on her birdlike shoulder. She removed it and placed it in her lap, knowing she must finish what she had started.

'I was sobbing hysterically when I reached the village. The first person I ran into was the German commandant. He pulled me into his office and questioned me with such ferociousness. I shall never forget the look of hatred in his eyes and the spit which flew at me as he shouted. I told him everything. Except about the piece of paper. I clutched my basket as if it were the side of a cliff and I was hanging over the sea. Instinct made me hide it and not reveal my secret. Immediately he jumped into a jeep with his men and stormed off. It was then I realised I may have condemned that poor pilot in some way. What happened to him? Was he imprisoned, was he shot? If I had kept quiet he might have escaped. I yearn to know what happened to him. I have never told anyone, but now I have been so ill it has made me seek the peace of mind of knowing what happened to that poor man that I betrayed.'

'Nana, do you still have the piece of paper?'

She leant down to reach a small beaded handbag at her feet, and handed Antonio a scrap of carefully folded paper.

'Hmm. It's just a man's name and a number. I guess so many men were lost in the war, he just wanted someone to know where he came down. We can try and trace him, but Nana, it's a long time ago.'

At that point Caroline felt it was right to speak. 'I have a friend who works for the Imperial War Museum in London. I could ask him if he could throw any light on this. It's the only thing I can think of.'

The old lady looked from one to the other of them. 'Would you? Would you please? I see him in my dreams . . . the blood . . . '

'Thank you, Caroline.' Antonio took her hand and held it. She knew she should pull away but she felt so connected to Antonio. Reluctantly, he released her. 'We appreciate your help. It has given us hope. Hasn't it, Nana?'

★ ★ ★

As Caroline strolled back to her room that evening, she put her hand to her cheek, imagining Antonio's touch soft as a prayer. She couldn't help thinking what a lovely family Antonio had. It would be so rewarding to be part of something as strong as that. *La famiglia* . . . she now understood what that well-known Italian phrase really meant.

Later Caroline, Mel and Izzy were sitting having drinks in the hotel bar. 'How did your date with Commissario Mazzotta go?' Caroline asked.

'Cesare is lovely. He looks forbidding doing his police work, very command-ing and forthright. But when you get to know him, he's funny. We had loads in common. He likes travelling and went all round Europe, Australia and the States before he joined the police. We chatted into the early hours.'

Caroline was just telling Mel and Izzy about her visit to Ischia and how beautiful all the flowers were there, when Oscar rolled up, full of the joys of spring. He ordered a bottle of Prosecco and joined them. Caroline was pleased to see a tan developing on his skin, which had been pale from spending too long trapped in an office. Laughter lines were gathering where there had been frown lines. He knew he had a whole week's holiday before him and going out with Kate had helped him to relax. These days he often spoke of her.

'Kate told me of an interesting development in the hunt for the person who stole from her shop. She says one of the coach party came in to tell her that she had noted down the numbers of all her banknotes, it's something she does whenever going on holiday in case her purse is stolen. She's passed the numbers to Commissario Mazzotta. I hope he can get people to look out for them, it could help trap the thief.' While he was speaking, a text bleeped through on his phone. 'Oh, and Caroline, a bit of news for you. Someone you know is coming out to Italy to join us for a day or two.'

'Who's that?' Caroline asked, feeling the bubbles from the wine fizz deliciously as they went down her throat.

'Peter. He has business in Naples. He's going to drop by. That's okay, isn't it? He and I are still friends.'

Caroline's throat constricted at the thought of seeing her ex-fiancé again. Her skin prickled, and she suddenly coughed, sitting up with alarm whilst Izzy thumped her on the back. 'Auntie Caro, are you okay?'

It was a while before Caroline could speak. Mel threw her a knowing look. Oscar, dear Oscar, what had he done? He always had her best interests at heart but was way off the mark on this one. He obviously thought she was lonely and missing Peter, when in fact it had been Antonio who had been plaguing Caroline's thoughts. The trouble with Oscar was he liked to sort things, and he never understood why they had split up. Men just didn't have a clue. A visit from Peter, for goodness' sake. How on earth would she cope with that? Oscar had been so kind to her in the past, she would just have to grin and bear it.

'That sounds nice,' she managed to say, her voice hollow in her own ears.

'Good, because he's coming here to the hotel to have dinner with us tomorrow.'

★　★　★

Caroline had an unsettled night, tossing and turning in her bed till she felt ragged. She couldn't contemplate breakfast but decided that a walk would clear her head. As she came up the hill back to the hotel, she heard someone running up behind her and encountered Antonio. With his shirt hanging out of his trousers, and his hair in disarray, he had obviously been rushing around madly.

'Antonio, is there something wrong?'

'Yes. Well, maybe,' he gasped, doubling over, his hands clutching his knees as he fought to get his breath back. 'It's Louisa. She's disappeared.'

'Disappeared?'

'Yes. She was to help with some stocktaking in the bar this morning. My father had ordered her to help more around the hotel. When she wasn't up at the due time, he stormed off to her bedroom. When he got there it was deserted, her bed hasn't been slept in. I've just been down to the beach; she sometimes goes there when she's upset. She's very hot-headed and things have been tense lately. But there's no sign of her. I don't know what to do, Caroline. She's been back late sometimes, even sneaked in through the window to avoid confronting Papa. But never stayed out all night.'

Caroline could see how agitated

Antonio was and that perhaps he wasn't thinking straight. 'Take me to her room, Antonio. Perhaps there will be clues there. Did you look for a note? Girls often write things down. Izzy keeps a diary and sometimes writes letters when she wants to get things off her chest.'

'You're right. I was too hasty. Let's go.'

The two of them ran. As they sped past the office, Salvatore was on the phone; he nodded, acknowledging them. 'Papa's ringing around all her friends. I should have searched her room before rushing off. I just felt her bed and it was cold and I panicked. Thank you, Caroline, you're the best person to have around in a crisis.'

Louisa's room was at the back of the hotel overlooking the garden. 'Were the French windows open like this?'

'Yes.'

'Antonio, there's broken china down here. Something's been smashed.'

'It's an ornament, given to her by my

mother. It was always by her bedside.'
She saw him look frantically around the
room, desperately searching for clues.
His gaze settled on the pink cushions,
on the soft toys with which Louisa had
brightened up her cosy retreat. She was
still so much a girl, so much a child,
despite her womanly looks. There
wasn't a note to be found.

'I'll get Izzy and Mel and we'll form a
search party.' Caroline was always
fiercely practical.

As they went out into the corridor,
they saw Salvatore come out of the lift.
His skin was grey, his step heavy as he
looked towards them. 'What on earth
am I going to do? None of her friends
has seen my little girl. Where can she
be?' Then, Salvatore let out a wail,
grabbed at his stomach, and they ran
over just in time for Antonio to catch
his father as his body collapsed in a
heap. 'Quickly,' Antonio appealed to
Caroline. 'Call the doctor.'

6

'There is too much acid in the stomach. Probably an ulcer. You must slow down, Salvatore.' Antonio and Caroline had helped a staggering Salvatore to his room. The doctor, an old family friend, had come immediately. His wife, a nurse, had come with him, and immediately set about rearranging Salvatore's pillows and administering medication.

Antonio placed a damp flannel on his father's forehead, trying to cool him as the day warmed relentlessly outside. Caroline had never been to Antonio's parents' suite of rooms at the Girasole. Unlike the plain walls in the rest of the hotel, Valentina had decorated this room in flowery unrestrained wallpaper with one wall full of family photographs — babies smiling, a mix of generations happy in each other's company.

The chest of drawers was laden with silver photo frames showing Valentina and Salvatore together, as young lovers, young marrieds and finally with their children — Antonio radiating movie-star looks and Louisa a blossoming beauty. They looked the perfect family unit. Yet here lay Salvatore, parted from Valentina by the deep waters of the Mediterranean while she looked after her ailing mother. Caroline had been waiting for her friend back in London to contact her with news about Nana Bonetti's English airman during the war. If only Caroline could sort out Nana Bonetti's worries, maybe Valentina could return where she belonged, by Salvatore's side.

Commissario Mazzotta arrived. Dark brows tensed heavy over his soulful eyes and lines of concentration etched deep between them. 'I am sorry to interrupt you on your sickbed, Salvatore, but the doctor says you are well enough to help with the investigation into Louisa's disappearance.'

Being an instinctively warm person, Caroline had reached out to hold Salvatore's hand. He had grasped it like a man in the water grasps a piece of wreckage to keep him afloat. 'While I have these two young people to give me strength,' Salvatore nodded to his son, acknowledging all that Antonio did for him, 'I will do everything necessary to find my daughter.'

'We *will* find her.' Commissario Mazzotta drew up a chair to be closer. 'I am determined to get to the bottom of this; the disappearance of one so young is a serious matter. Am I right in thinking Louisa's bed wasn't slept in, and none of her friends know where she is?'

'That is correct.' Salvatore sipped from a glass of iced water Caroline held for him.

'And that you two have searched her room and there is no note, only a smashed ornament and the French windows open?'

'Yes.'

'Is there a CCTV camera near Louisa's room?'

'No,' replied Salvatore, 'only at the front of the hotel.'

'We can still check any footage for clues. Please have your staff make it available. Who was the last person to see Louisa?'

'She was out with friends yesterday evening,' Antonio replied. 'The receptionist on the front desk would have seen her if she returned by the main entrance, but it is possible she entered her room directly from the back of the hotel; she would often go round through the French doors.'

Commissario Mazzotta rubbed his hand across his chin. Something was troubling him. 'I would like to see her bedroom.'

'Of course.' Antonio went to the door. 'No, Papa, you are too ill, you must stay and rest.'

'Come now, Salvatore,' the nurse said. 'Try and relax.'

Antonio and Caroline escorted the

Commissario to Louisa's room. He looked through her wardrobe and drawers. All seemed in order, but the smashed ornament made him frown. 'We will have the pieces dusted for fingerprints and the windows. Although if someone had hidden, knowing she often let herself in through the back, they could easily have waited for her to open the French doors. Then they could force their way in behind. This would gain them entry without leaving any clues. Such a scenario may account for the broken ornament. If it was very special to Louisa, it is unlikely she would have broken it, but they may have done it to menace her into going with them.'

'They? Why are you assuming anyone else was involved and she hasn't just gone off in a huff?' Antonio looked shocked, and as if he would happily go out right now and fight anyone who had harmed Louisa.

'I do not want to alarm you, and I wouldn't yet mention it in front of your father, but there have been two incidents down this coast in the last six months of attempted kidnappings from wealthy families.'

'Kidnapping,' Caroline gasped.

'But we are far from wealthy.' Antonio was pacing up and down. 'My father is a good businessman but he doesn't have a fortune.'

'Unfortunately the abductors may not know that. Their first attempt was to take a child from one of the large yachts moored in the bay. The second time, they became more audacious and broke into the residence of a television executive who has a holiday home and a new baby. Luckily his live-in chauffeur disturbed them and they fled. Obviously we will carry out a full investigation, but I cannot help thinking this gang may have struck again and this time been more successful.'

As they walked back into Salvatore's bedroom, having resolved at present not to worry him with such suspicions, the Commmissario asked Salvatore some last questions. 'Can you think of any people who might not have Louisa's best interests at heart?'

'I certainly can.' Salvatore was lying with his head on the pillow, but there was still fire in his belly and determination in his stare. 'Firstly, there is that boy who has been hanging around her. He is a no-good ruffian. He and his friends may have something to do with this. Then there is that old devil Casiraghi up the hill. We have recently had a dispute over land. In his younger days there was talk he had links to the Mafia; those men stop at nothing to get what they want.'

'Father, really, you mustn't slander Senor Casiraghi. I'm sure he had nothing to do with Louisa's disappearance.'

'I wouldn't be so sure. We are at war, he and I.' The nurse had rinsed out and replaced the flannel on Salvatore's forehead to calm him down. He closed his eyes and clutched his hand to his stomach.

The doctor shook his head, indicating that they should stop, but there was a steely determination to Commissario Mazzotta's pursuit of the truth. 'I am truly sorry to tire you, but the first twenty-four hours after such a disappearance are crucial. The work done now makes all the difference in finding out who has done this. I have one more question. Does anyone know the whereabouts of Louisa's mobile phone? All teenagers have one nowadays and I didn't see it in her room. If we can track the signals it may help locate her. I will get onto my technical people.'

'She is always glued to it, it's like a third arm,' said Antonio. 'She must have it with her.' They looked to Salvatore in case he could shed any light on the matter, but he had drifted off into a troubled sleep.

'Let us leave him now to get some rest.' Commissario Mazzotta ushered Antonio and Caroline out into the corridor. 'One other thing. We have a lead on the theft of money at Kate

Weston's shop. I would be grateful if you could pass on to her that we have traced the owner of the raincoat the thief was wearing; you remember, the one with the strange belt that was not the original.'

'That means you have found the thief then.' Antonio's voice brightened.

'Not so fast, I'm afraid. A regular visitor to your hotel, one of the suppliers who drops off truffles to your chef, left it here by mistake and was asking for it. If only she could remember where exactly she left it, that will give us a useful lead. She was so busy that day rushing from one hotel to the next she has not been much use. But often when people are not trying to remember, they will recall. Also two of the euro notes that were stolen have turned up in one of the banks. Two of my men are trying to trace which shops banked them so that we can try and find out who spent them. I will report back as soon as I find anything out. If it is permissible, I will call in on Mel and

Izzy before I leave. I will ask Izzy gently about anything Louisa said which may give a clue to her disappearance. Often with abductions, someone will have been followed beforehand, and Izzy may be able to tell us if Louisa mentioned anything along those lines.'

So saying, Cesare Mazzotta left, and Caroline suspected that dropping in on Mel would give him some much-needed light relief. They had been seeing a lot of one another lately and had come to be viewed as a couple around the hotel. Mel had attended family meals and met Cesare's parents and brothers and sisters, who had greeted her with open arms. Caroline strongly suspected that they were eager to see Cesare settled, and Mel with her caring ways would be good for a man with such a demanding job.

With Salvatore laid up, it was Antonio's job to run the hotel. He stepped in admirably, flying around, encouraging the kitchen staff and sorting out problems in the office.

'Whatever we do, Caroline, we must keep the hotel functioning like clockwork. What with the theft from Kate Weston's shop and now this, I am very anxious that we keep going as normal and do not attract bad publicity to the Girasole. That sort of thing can lead to cancelled bookings, which would break my father's heart. I will alert my mother to the problems we are having, but I will minimise them and just tell her that Louisa has gone away with friends.'

'Do you think that's best?' asked Caroline. 'Doesn't your mother have a right to know what's really happened?'

Antonio raked his fingers through his fringe, then held Caroline's hand tight. 'It is what my father would do. He would be strong for everybody. At the moment there is nothing Mama could do to help here. The Commissario is on the case and is a clever man. The doctor says my father will recover and he is being nursed night and day. I cannot land my poor mother with any more trouble. If the situation is not better by tomorrow I will tell Mama the truth. This evening, I am going to go myself and search the places where Louisa goes out with her friends, and see if I can discover anything from them.'

Caroline was impressed by Antonio's taking control and his presence of mind in a crisis, not allowing anyone to panic. He even managed to calm Izzy, who was troubled at Louisa's disappearance. Neither of them mentioned to her any suspicions of kidnapping.

'What do you think's happened to Louisa? She is safe, isn't she?'

'Of course she is, little one. Any moment now she will phone us and apologise. She will maybe have been out late and slept over at a friend's, and simply have forgotten to let us know.'

Izzy looked doubtful. 'But maybe she went swimming, like you did, Antonio, and got stuck on the rocks or something. Is it okay, Auntie Caro, if Rafaele and I spend the day down in Paulo Bay, and go up the hill and look out to sea, just in case? Beatrice will be able to see us from her house in the lemon grove. We won't go out of sight and she's said I can stay for dinner. Rafaele wants to be like Detective Mazzotta when he leaves school. Maybe he can help find Louisa like a real detective.'

'Only if you are very careful and stay by Rafaele's side and don't go swimming. If you want to swim, come back here to the hotel pool, it's safer,' ordered Caroline.

Caroline would have spent the day worrying about the arrival of her ex-fiancé Peter had it not been for all the other things on her mind. Just as she was rushing upstairs to get ready for dinner with him and Oscar, the head waiter came past, a scowl on his normally friendly features.

'Is there a problem?' asked Caroline. With Antonio off speaking to Louisa's friends, and Salvatore laid up in bed, the staff had come to look on her as an honorary family member. Her natural managerial abilities meant she was happy to deal with any problems.

'Sophia has called in sick, just before dinner. It is intolerable, that girl is getting unreliable as well as sullen.' Caroline felt sorry for her, knowing of the waitress's pregnancy and the reason she hadn't revealed it — because she was anxious she might lose her job. She resolved to speak to Sophia as soon as she returned, and sort the situation out.

'Don't worry, I can ring one of the other girls and ask her to come in. She was asking Antonio for extra shifts the other day.' Having sorted that problem, Caroline barely had time to get ready, or to worry about how uncomfortable things might be on seeing Peter for the first time since their split. She had only time for the merest hint of makeup, a simple sky-blue dress and her hair gathered into a tousled updo.

Caroline was grateful that Antonio was out when they sat down to dinner. She had resolved to have no relationship at present and Antonio wasn't her boyfriend; still, it might have been awkward to be with those two young men together. Oscar told Peter about Louisa's disappearance, and that gave the three of them a topic of conversation and a diversion.

After dinner, it being a warm evening, she, Peter and Oscar wandered down to Paulo Bay. 'How are your family, Peter, your mother and father?' The dinner really hadn't been as difficult as Caroline had feared, and conversation was flowing. Caroline had been fond of Peter's parents and was pleased for an update. Peter laughed and her heart lurched to hear him. That was one of the things that had been so attractive about him. He was a man you would often hear laughing with someone, telling a joke or recounting a funny story well before he arrived in a room. 'They're well, thank you. My father is continuing his nightly battle with slugs in the garden.' Peter was a born raconteur and his stories about his father's continuing fight with garden pests, and the many contraptions he built to ward them off, had them enjoying his company more than ever.

Suddenly, Caroline felt relaxed for the first time that day as she listened to the waves lap the shore, and recalled how wonderful things had been when she and Peter were first together. He would make such an effort to please her — like he was doing now.

Lights out in the bay of Naples twinkled. Their feet crunched on the pebbles. Suddenly, Oscar's mobile phone ringing disturbed the scene. He chatted quickly then said, 'I have to go back to the hotel and make a call and check some papers. It's work, I'm afraid.'

'Really, Oscar. Do you have to?' Caroline asked.

'Sorry. Peter will look after you.'

Oscar shot off as usual. He was the one who had made this reunion come about and now he had deserted them. But Caroline couldn't be cross with him. She found that now the ice had been broken, she didn't dread being alone with Peter. She had forgotten how effortlessly charming he was, and how easy on the eye in his smart lounge suit.

They strolled towards the boatyard. 'I have an idea,' said Peter with an impish grin as he looked at the boats for hire with their fluttering flags and fairy lights wound round their masts. Within moments he had taken out his wallet, exchanged a bunch of euros with one of the owners, and before she knew it, they were taking a boat trip on the gentle bay. It was gorgeous, the calmest of seas, with Mount Vesuvius brooding majestically in the distance and lights from the houses on the hillside twinkling like cats' eyes.

'I'm glad we've got a little time alone together.' Peter stood at a distance from her, careful not to invade her space. The breeze tickled a tendril of hair and she pushed it behind her ear. He took a deep breath and continued. 'We never really talked about the break-up, did we? I wrote you that one letter but I never had the courage to say sorry properly. I wish I had. Caroline, I am really sorry. Sorry that I tried to tell you what to do, that I wasn't sensitive to the freedom you needed.'

Tall and commanding though he was, with classically handsome features like a young Paul Newman, Peter looked at this moment like a forlorn schoolboy. She got the impression he had been composing this speech for some time. Caroline felt her heart melting like ice cream on a summer day. She took a step towards him. She had never hated him, never wanted him to feel bad. In the distance from the bar on the shore came the sound of Neapolitan love songs played on a violin.

'I wasn't as good as I should have been. I wasn't as kind.'

'You weren't unkind, Peter, just old-fashioned in the way you see relationships.' She suddenly saw the need in him, a need to be loved.

'I know, I was too much like my father. Too commanding, too much the darned alpha male, always having to prove I knew best. I so regret that. I've changed, Caroline.' He raised his head and looked at her with gorgeous blue eyes. 'I've had a good long time to think. You were everything to me. There's a part of me missing since I lost you. We made so many plans, didn't we? A beautiful house in the country, a flat in town, babies, children, a cat and a dog. A proper home. There's no one else I want those things with and there never will be. I love you with all my heart. I realise now you needed your own career, to be your own person, and I can give you that freedom, I promise. I was selfish. But I can change. I *will* change if you'll give me another chance.'

Caroline felt tears prick the back of her eyes. So many times after the break-up she had gone over in her head the things she wanted to hear from Peter. Finally, they had been given this magical moonlit night. Romantic music played in the background and the little boat chugged along under the Italian stars, and here was Peter, the love of her life, saying all the things she had wanted to hear so badly.

'Let me show you, Caroline, I can be the man you want. You look utterly beautiful tonight, so lovely, you take my breath away. I was a fool to ever let you go. You're one of the kindest people I've ever met. If a man makes a mistake, isn't it fair to let him try again?'

He had moved closer, was standing next to her, towering and protective, the way he used to be. Her heart pounded in her ears. She could feel the warmth of his body heating her skin. Suddenly it felt as if this was meant to be. That it was the thing she had been waiting for. If Peter really was willing to change, if he had seen the error of his ways, then that would mend her broken heart. He was so much the man she had always wanted. If he could learn to respect her freedom, allow her to have her career and not be in control of her, then it would work.

He certainly seemed to want that.

It felt as if a circle had been completed, as if the sorry mess of their broken engagement could somehow be soldered back together like a golden ring which, broken, had been made to look like new. At that moment he was promising her everything she had wanted so badly all these months. She'd be crazy not to try again, wouldn't she?

He was standing so close. He ran his hands up her bare arms, making her tingle. Her breaths came short and fast. 'Darling, it's been so long.' His voice, deep and sensual, resonated through her body. He encircled her in his arms. She looked up and eyes as blue as the depths of the ocean looked down, imploring her, as if she could see into his soul. His need for her took her breath away as he oh-so-softly pushed his fingers into her hair and brought his lips down to kiss her. She was powerless to resist. He had always been like a bewitching drug to her and she succumbed. Her head swam, her knees threatened to fail her; but if they had, it wouldn't have mattered because he held her so tight, so firm, it was as if he was carrying her as she released herself totally to him. Her hair, soft in the breeze, entwined with his, as if they were one. All the old feelings of want resurfaced, all the regret that things had gone wrong began to be buried.

When they came out of the kiss, he tenderly placed his forehead against hers, and she could feel him trembling. Her hand felt tiny in his. 'What do you say, Caroline? Can we try again?'

'These few days that you're here in Italy. Yes,' she nodded. 'Let's give us one more chance to make it work.'

★　★　★

Antonio was tending to the flowers outside the front of the hotel. He had paperwork to do inside, but being here raking round the soil, drinking in the vibrant oranges and yellows of the bougainvillea, was good for the soul.

And he was indeed having to do some soul-searching today. He had been eating a hearty breakfast until he had been called away to take a call from the Professore. This was the news he had been waiting for. Days ago, he had been told that he was running neck and neck with the American student for a place helping dig out the last ruins of Pompeii. In fact, one of the committee had come up to him when he was studying in the library last week and whispered, 'My money is on you, young di Labati. The American is full of confidence and his father has money, but you are the one who pores over his books and writes sparkling words on the ancient world. You would inspire future generations.'

The whispered speech and a wink of encouragement had given him hope. When the Professore's call came five minutes ago, he had grasped the phone tight, his palms sweating in anticipation.

'My boy.' The voice was jovial as

always. But there was an edge to it. Antonio gripped the arms of his seat. He wanted this so much it hurt. 'The Committee has given its judgement. I am afraid Rick McPartlin has been chosen. It is a crime. You were clearly the brighter student with inspiring ideas, but I fear the American's wealth trumped all that. His father has promised an immense donation. Funding is so hard to come by. I am sorry, Antonio. I hope you will continue your studies and not do anything foolish like give up your place in my class.'

Antonio had found it difficult to speak. He'd mumbled a choked thanks to the Professore, then gone straight outside. It felt as if the world had stopped turning. So, this was his destiny. Pulling up weeds and standing in for his father at the Girasole. He felt as if his feet were manacled to the soil.

Just as he was about to attack a particularly pernicious weed, young Rafaele breezed up the road, whistling. Round his neck hung a pair of binoculars. In his hands he carried a magnifying glass and a notebook. How lovely to be so carefree, so full of hope, thought Antonio.

'You look busy, Antonio, always working hard at the hotel, making it look lovely.'

Antonio couldn't bear to look back at the Girasole; he wanted to run and escape from it forever. 'What are you up to, Rafaele?'

'I am detecting. Izzy and I are off to look for Louisa again. You haven't heard anything, have you?'

'No.'

'I shall be like Sherlock Holmes. Izzy has told me about the great English detective. How he approaches everything very logically, and how he learns things by observing. I was observing yesterday.'

'You were?' Antonio tried to sound interested.

'Yes. Commissario Mazzotta went to speak to Signor Casiraghi. We heard what they said; we were in the bushes searching for evidence, and suddenly they came by, so we crouched down. Signor Casiraghi told them that Louisa and your father had a huge fight the day she disappeared. Something about her phone, we couldn't catch the rest. I don't like Senor Casiraghi; he seemed to be trying to put the blame on your Papa.'

'Only to steer blame away from himself and his cronies.' Antonio felt his blood boil. The more he learnt about his neighbour, the more he started to think that Salvatore's suspicions about him being involved in Louisa's disappearance might be well-founded. His enmity against their family seemed to know no bounds.

'I am determined to help Commissario Mazzotta. I'm sure I can find stuff out, I know this area better than him and his policemen. Here's Izzy now. We're off back to the beach again. We are going to check on all the boats. Bye now.'

Antonio started to clean his hands of

soil. His father had had a restless night and he wanted to let him sleep in, but he should go off and find out about this latest argument with Louisa. Just as he was gathering his rake and hoe, Caroline turned up.

She looked especially lovely today in a dress of soft pink lace. Just looking at her was like a balm to all his wounds. He had not seen her all yesterday evening; it was almost as if she were trying to avoid him. And when he gave her a cheery hello and beckoned her over, she seemed uneasy. The one chink of light on Antonio's horizon was that Caroline had suggested they run gourmet cooking classes to help promote the hotel. She had been so enthusiastic last week when they'd been planning it; she said it gave her something constructive to do whilst the builders were taking so long on La Casa. She had talked it all through with Beatrice before approaching Salvatore, as the classes were to be led by Beatrice at her house in the lemon grove.

Rafaele's mother and grandmother would be grateful for the extra income and it would give guests something fun to do without travelling far from the hotel. Caroline was so entrepreneurial and Antonio had loved seeing her face light up as her ideas were developed. The more she got involved in the hotel, the more he hoped she might stay on after work on La Casa was finished, and that, perhaps, she might come around to going out with him.

'Caroline, good morning. How are you? I had some new thoughts on your idea of the cooking classes. Might we talk about it over a morning coffee?'

'I would have loved to.' Her pretty eyes wouldn't meet his. What was going on? 'But I'm booked for today. I'm going out. With . . . with Peter.'

At that moment, a top-of-the-range hire care drew up, with a man at the wheel so suave and polished in his designer shirt and jeans he could easily have been one of the millionaires who kept their fancy yachts in the harbour.

He got out, giving Antonio barely a glance, as if to say he was only a gardener, and ushered Caroline into the car. She gave Antonio a fond but low-key wave goodbye. In a whoosh of dust they were gone.

Antonio had been trumped twice that morning. But the thing that hurt most was to see Caroline with Peter, a man totally out of Antonio's league. How could he compete with a rich man who had a golden future? Two of his dreams had turned to dust today, and he felt as if he, too, could simply disintegrate on the spot.

But he set his jaw square and he made himself stand tall. He remembered his beloved grandmother telling them of all the privations she had been through in the war, and yet she had kept strong. She had always helped to give him strength and he mustn't crumble now.

He went back downstairs and approached the office with new resolve. He must think very carefully about his future now that his dreams at Pompeii were not to be realised. He owed it to his mother and father to make a success of the hotel. That was all that was left to him. What's more, as head of the family with Salvatore ill, it was his duty to do everything possible to discover what had happened to his sister. The worst thing for his family now would be for him to moon about over lost hopes. He must be decisive. There were bills to be paid, supplies to order in, people's wages to sort out. So many people depended upon him. A pile of post awaited him. With a sigh, he went to it with a will.

Firstly, there was a letter all the way from London, addressed to Caroline with the postmark of the Imperial War Museum. Of course — that would be the answer about the airman who had landed in the war whom his grandmother was so worried about. He itched to know what it held, but would have to wait until Caroline returned. He was quite distracted when he came to the last letter addressed to his father, but as soon as he read the first line, he felt as if an earthquake had struck under his feet.

WE HAVE YOUR DAUGHTER. SHE IS SAFE. PUT 20,000 EUROS INTO A HOLDALL AND AWAIT FURTHER INSTRUCTIONS. IF YOU WANT TO SEE LOUISA AGAIN DO NOT TELL THE POLICE. WE WILL BE IN TOUCH.

Antonio stared at the letter in horror. Twenty thousand euros; where on earth would he get money like that? And should he tell the police or not? His sister was in danger. Now, more than ever, he needed Caroline, desperately.

7

Antonio felt tortured. He stuffed the ransom letter into his pocket.

'Have you heard anything from Louisa, or from the police?' the cleaner polishing the lobby asked.

'Er, no,' stammered Antonio, the letter burning against his side. What was he to do? He could barely concentrate; everywhere he turned, people asked about his dilemma. To distract himself, he went to the kitchens to check on meal preparations. The chef immediately put down a large tray he was carrying. 'You look worried, Mr di Labati, I hope it's not bad news about Louisa.'

'No, I've heard nothing,' lied Antonio, getting out of the busy man's way.

How could he possibly have any peace from his problems? His head was hammering. Escaping upstairs into the garden, he paced up and down past the roses. He'd phoned the bank the moment he read the letter. They'd advance him the money, but it wouldn't be available until tomorrow. Would the people who'd taken Louisa wait that long, would they give him time?

Way down the end of the garden, set in an alcove in the old stone wall, was a nook. Antonio opened its little glass doors to reveal a serene Madonna holding a tiny baby. She had on a blue cloak and white robe, caught around her waist with a gold cord. Both mother and child wore tiny golden crowns. Antonio had brought his troubles to the figure in this little shrine since he was a boy. He picked a handful of oxeye daisies. Removing a bunch of faded lavender flowers, he remembered they had been placed in the vase by his sister last week. He didn't have the heart to discard them.

Instead, he laid Louisa's flowers at the foot of the Madonna. A whiff of lavender scent came to him like a memory of his vibrant sibling. Putting the daisies in their place, he prayed hard he was doing the right thing in not telling the police about the letter. What if Louisa's abductors were watching the hotel and saw the Commissario turn up? They might get spooked and do something terrible to his beloved sister, and it would all be his fault.

'Please send me a sign, sweet Madonna, that I am doing the right thing. I don't know which way to turn.'

That moment, as if in answer, Antonio heard the roar of an expensive engine. He turned to see Peter speed to a halt then climb out of his hire car. The Englishman opened the door for Caroline. The two stood smiling and sharing confidences as lovers do. Antonio couldn't look, couldn't bear to see them kiss. He heard the car roar off; no doubt Peter, with his many business dealings, had important work to do. Antonio forced himself to look; he must accept reality. Caroline gazed lingeringly at the departing car; she must be so in love. It tore Antonio in two. He bit his lip, closed the doors to the shrine and set off for the bar. Keeping busy was the only way out of this misery.

As he approached the bar, one of the receptionists came up to him looking distraught. 'Has anything been heard from your sister?'

'No.'

'Oh dear, I was hoping there might be good news, because I have bad news, I'm afraid.'

'What is it?'

Caroline appeared at that moment. She wandered over as the receptionist said, 'The party of Canadians due tomorrow have cancelled their booking.'

'Cancelled?' Antonio gasped. 'There must be some mistake, that's our biggest booking this month, twenty double rooms.'

'I know. It's dreadful. What will your poor father say? I felt sick when I took the call.'

'Why have they pulled out?'

'The tour operator heard about money disappearing from the hotel. Bad news travels fast. He's panicked and booked his party elsewhere. He's refusing to pay the cancellation fees, saying he cannot possibly send his guests to a hotel where their belongings mightn't be safe.'

'Oh, Antonio.' Caroline looked as troubled for him as if she had been part-owner of the hotel. Her presence was the one silver lining around so many dark clouds.

Antonio ran his fingers exasperatedly through his mop of hair. 'I will speak to him, try and change his mind.'

'Can't I help?' asked Caroline. 'You look done in, Antonio. Still no news about Louisa?'

Antonio was on the verge of telling Caroline about the letter, but feared the consequences and thought better of it. 'No,' he answered weakly. He hated lying, even if only by omission.

She pondered for a moment, then said, 'I used to work in PR, and our job was to turn things around. I've an idea. How would it be if we invited the Canadians' tour operator here now for coffee with some of our chef's special Easter cake, and ask Geraldo Bonomi to join us. He's had two groups of tourists stay here in the short time I've been at the Girasole, and he was glowing in his praise. Maybe if your Canadian operator sits with us for a while, Geraldo can help us sweet-talk him. Giulietta, please could you speak to the kitchen and get something organised for an hour's time, and I'll arrange it all with Geraldo.'

The girl shot off, only too pleased to do something practical. Antonio went to talk to the Canadian tour operator. While Antonio was in the office, Giulietta came back seeking Caroline out.

'Before you call Geraldo, there's something else I didn't want to mention when Antonio was here; he has enough to deal with. Sophia the waitress has phoned in sick. Again. That woman's always in crisis.'

Caroline didn't know what to say. She felt sorry for Sophia, it must be awful knowing you were pregnant and being fearful of losing your job. She'd meant to call on Sophia but hadn't had time.

'Between you and me,' whispered Giulietta, 'her husband's in trouble.'

'Trouble?'

'I hear rumours he bought a boat, quite an overpriced one because he had a good well-paid job. Then there were unexpected redundancies. Now he can't sell it, and can't afford to run it. I think that's what's making Sophia ill.'

Poor Sophia; it was even worse than Caroline had thought. 'I must go and visit, please get me her address when you have a minute.' Caroline added the task to her mental to-do list, but the most pressing thing was to phone Geraldo.

'My dear,' the Italian was effusive and obviously a fan of Caroline's, 'for you, *bella donna*, anything. It's not difficult for me to wax lyrical about the Girasole. It's the best family-run hotel along this coast. I'd like to help out Antonio and Salvatore. This problem with Louisa must be awful for them. I'll come right over.'

The four of them sat together and the chef laid out an Easter treat in the sun-filled lounge. The traditional dove-shaped Columba Pasquale cake, topped with delectable crunchy Sicilian pizzuta almonds and still warm from the oven, was a total hit. It disappeared with only crumbs left behind. Geraldo was as good as his word, helping everyone to extra espresso and being thoroughly persuasive. 'So,' he said, licking his fingers and holding his round tummy in satisfaction, 'you see what a wonderful time your Canadians will have here if only you can see some way to changing your mind. The chef is among the best in the region. I've been sending guests to the Girasole for the last twenty years. Antonio and Salvatore look after visitors like honoured VIPs. The Girasole has a blemish-free record, there's never been any trouble here; not like in some hotels closer to town, oh, the stories I could tell you. Please don't let a one-off incident get out of proportion.'

'Also,' Caroline piped up, 'we're thinking of holding cookery courses. They'll be at the farmhouse of a local lemon grove down the road. Your guests could be the first to try them. I'm sure we could do a very competitive rate. The first one might even be free to your Canadians.'

The tour operator shrugged his shoulders and threw up his hands. 'Maybe I was too hasty. You have persuaded me by a mixture of shame-less bribery and sheer common sense.' He stood up and bid them all farewell, before setting off with another of the chef's Easter cakes wrapped up in foil to take home to his family.

When they'd thanked Geraldo and waved him off, Antonio beckoned Caroline to sit down beside him. He wished he could reach out and hug her; she had been so enthusiastic and spirited, a superb advocate for the hotel.

But she brushed off his thanks. 'You need help at this difficult time, Antonio, with all the stuff that's going on. I don't know how you're coping. I felt awful when you started talking to me about the cookery courses this morning and I had to run off. I didn't want to sound rude, but Peter had planned something special. Is there anything else up, Antonio? You look pale; you're not ill are you?'

He couldn't tell her he was sick in his heart at seeing her with Peter. But he needed to share with someone the awful truth of the ransom letter. He drew it out and handed it to her. 'What shall I do?'

Caroline was unequivocal. 'You must tell the police immediately.'

'I'm not so sure.'

'Please, Antonio. The Commissario will know what to do, he'll be used to threats from evil people. He'll be discreet.'

'It's good to share it with somebody. I didn't know what to do. I can't confide in my father and make him more ill, and I can't land the problem on my mother when she's miles away in Ischia having to care for my grandmother.'

'It's high time you let your mother know about Louisa's disappearance. You can't carry the weight of all this responsibility alone. Anyway, it's her right to know. How about if your Nana came back here to the Girasole to stay for a while? Your Nana could sit with your father and they could keep each other company. Isn't that what you Italians mean by *la famiglia*, pulling together and supporting each other?'

'I suppose it's a possibility. They get on well and Papa is bored on his own.' Suddenly Antonio felt energised. He jumped up. 'I will phone the Commissario about the letter right now. Then the two of us can sit down and organise a cookery day for the Canadians the day after tomorrow. The distraction of it might help me cope. Life has to go on, doesn't it?'

'That'd be brilliant. I've almost got things planned in my head. As well as the cookery, you could give people a talk on food and the Romans. All the things you told me at Pompeii were fascinating. We can get food in for a practice run this evening, then all we have to do is refine things. We'll try the talks out on Kate and Oscar. Oscar never cooks anything and Kate doesn't look terribly domesticated. We'll choose something easy, they can join in, and we'll all eat the dish together afterwards. If they enjoy it, the Canadians will. I'll speak to Beatrice and sort it.'

Antonio dialled the Commissario but the detective had a day off. His men would contact him once they tracked him down. When Antonio told Caroline, who was already sitting in the lounge, writing out recipes and shopping lists, her eyes lit up.

'Of course he's off today. I know where he is, he offered to take Mel out to lunch. They'll have finished and be enjoying a long leisurely coffee. I'm always amazed how you Italians can take all day over lunch.'

'Do you think it's right to disturb them? They seem to be getting on incredibly well these days.' Antonio had a smile on his lips for the first time that day.

'True, he does seem happiest when he's in Mel's company. But his work is vital to him. I'm sure he'll be fine if we go over now. He did tell us to let him know any time if we had news of Louisa. Have you got your car keys?'

They drove into the hills and talked about the gourmet days. After visiting Italy, the Canadians were spending a week in London. One of the things they were keen to see was an exhibition at the British Museum called 'Life and Death in Pompeii'. Antonio's talk after the cookery lesson would include slides of the exhibits — he'd helped prepare them to be shipped over to London. It would be a real coup for the holiday-makers to speak to one of the experts involved in the exhibition before seeing it themselves.

Cesare Mazzotta's favourite restaurant was a family-run *trattoria* off the steep road above the Girasole — it was owned by one of his best friends. Tables lined a terrace overlooking the Bay of Naples. Grape vines entwined over the wooden pergola to give diners shade from what had been a baking hot day. Caroline was glad of the cool green leaves and sea breeze. She'd spent all morning with Peter driving to Positano with the roof on the car down. She'd had too many UV rays today and was pleased she'd taken her sun hat and sunglasses with her. Peter had pooh-poohed her gentle urging to put the roof up, knowing best as always, even though the back of his neck was red when they returned. 'I've got loads of sun cream on, don't fuss. Besides, I've always had this fantasy of hiring a top-of-the-range open car and driving along Mediterranean roads. It's so exhilarating. Do this in England and you'd freeze to death.'

Down on the restaurant terrace, deep in conversation, Mel and Cesare sat staring into one another's eyes. The detective was holding her hands. Caroline felt a little bad at disturbing them, but Cesare seemed pleased to see her and Antonio. 'Ah, my good friends, come and join us.'

'I'm afraid this isn't a courtesy call.' Antonio took Cesare aside to show him the ransom letter, while Mel and Caroline went off to the ladies' room.

'You look flushed, Mel, have you caught the sun today too?'

'It's not that. It's Cesare. He's asked me to give up my job with Oscar and stay here in Sorrento.'

'Heavens. I knew he was keen on you, but that sounds like serious stuff. It'd be a big step.'

'It would. But, well, I have to admit I've been smitten since the first day I

215

saw him. He's so strong in every way, such a good man. He makes me go weak at the knees.' She giggled. 'The only thing that worries me is that we've known each other such a short time. I don't know . . . I think I love him.' She shook her head in bewilderment. 'But it's all happening so fast. Besides, I've been wondering for a while now how much Oscar and Izzy still need me. Did you know that Kate Weston's estranged husband has asked her for a divorce? They've been separated for ages but now it's going to be final. If things go well, Oscar and she may get together for good. Izzy's more independent now. I've often considered what I'll do when they don't need me any longer. Oh, Caroline, I don't know what to say to Cesare. He's mentioned a work colleague who's looking for a nanny for their newborn. If it works out between us, he'd . . . well, he's asked me to marry him. He wants a long engagement, but once we're sure, he'd like to start a family. Children are very important to him and he's been neglecting his personal life. Last year he was promoted. Now he wants to sort his future. He doesn't want to be alone forever. I don't know what to say.'

'So what did you say?'

'I told him I'd think about it, that I hadn't expected his offer but I was very flattered. That seemed to be enough for now. He's too gentlemanly to push. He said he'd wait forever for me. No man's ever told me that.' Mel looked her prettiest, flushed with excitement, and Caroline could easily see how she'd won the detective's heart. 'Enough of me. How was your date with Peter?'

'It was lovely but too hot. He was sweet, very caring, wanting to stop and show me every wine producer and beautiful view. He's trying really hard. He's texted me three times since we parted. I haven't had a chance to reply, though, I've been busy with Antonio.' She told Mel about their plans for the gourmet days and about the ransom letter.

'Poor Antonio, he must be terrified, Louisa's life is in his hands.'

Caroline's phone bleeped again. Another text from Peter; this time saying that he didn't feel good, it might be something he ate, and he'd phone later.

Commissario Mazzotta made his apologies to Mel and sped off to have the ransom letter analysed for fingerprints. There was little else they could do, so they went back to the hotel.

'By the way,' said Antonio as they entered the office, 'you received this letter from London.'

Caroline tore it open. 'It's from my friend at the Imperial War Museum. He's traced your Nana's airman. It's fabulous news. The airman's alive and well and living in Northampton; also he's a well-known member of an online group of ex-servicemen. My friend contacted him and told him of your Nana's concerns, and he's sent this lovely reply; and, see here, a photograph of him with his huge family. He's elderly now and living in an old people's home, but was touched to hear of her concern. He's desperate for her to know how he thrived and prospered after the war.'

'What a relief.' Antonio brushed away a skein of hair from his forehead. 'It's a huge weight off my shoulders and it will be for my Nana too. I shall phone Mama right now and tell her the good news. She's been wanting to come back to the Girasole for ages, she's really homesick. Maybe she might return as early as tomorrow and bring my Nana back with her. I feel so relieved, and it's all down to you. You may even have helped save my father's beloved hotel. The last thing we need in this recession is lost business.'

'Nonsense,' Caroline blushed under his praise. Just for a moment, she wondered how she would feel if Antonio were to make the same sort of offer Cesare had made Mel. Her heart ached, as if pulled two ways. Then she pushed thoughts of Antonio out of her mind. Her destiny lay with Peter. Surely he was the man who deserved her love and devotion; after all, hadn't he travelled all the way here to take her back to London where she belonged?

★　★　★

Oscar and Kate stood joshing each other in Beatrice's kitchen that evening, pretending to be Canadian tourists. Ingredients lay in front of them, together with a bound booklet of recipes Caroline had made with photos of the Girasole and Beatrice's beautiful garden.

Caroline was concerned about Antonio. Normally smart, his shirt was unironed and his hair awry. This business with his sister was taking such a toll. She only hoped that an evening doing something completely different might take his mind off it. Kate and Oscar knew nothing of the ransom letter as Antonio wanted to keep things quiet. There had been silence from the kidnappers. Antonio was in limbo, and a very lost soul he looked too. Caroline took a deep breath, and started reading from the notes she'd written of her practice presentation.

'Today,' Caroline announced as if she were talking to an audience of twenty Canadians rather than two giggly English people, 'Beatrice is going to show us an Italian classic — *zabaglione*.'

'Hey, that's a bit of a mouthful.' Oscar put on an excellent Canadian accent. Kate joined in the fun, doing the same. She batted her eyelashes at him.

'Hopefully it will be darrrling if you let the nice lady tell us how.'

'Of course, my little domestic goddess,' sang Oscar, looking comical in his pinny, standing to attention, wooden spoon brandished like a sword.

Beatrice didn't let their joking distract her. She was a natural. Her soft Italian accent was stronger when she was addressing an audience. 'First we plunge our peaches in boiling water.

Then we pops them into iced water. That makes it easier for us to get the skeens off.'

Beatrice peeled off the velvet skins and chopped the fruit whilst her Mama cleared away the leavings, buzzing around and wiping the table.

'I don't think this is so good for my manicure,' joked Kate in her Saskatchewan drawl.

Beatrice tried not to giggle. 'We poach the peaches with water and sugar. Then we add a secret ingredient, fragrant lemon verbena leaves from my garden.'

'Mmm, those are really pungent.' Caroline rubbed one between her fingers and passed it to Antonio to sample the scent.

'Italian cooking ees all about giving things time.' Caroline could see even Oscar and Kate were fascinated by the presentation; it was so full of warmth and passion, it couldn't fail to wow the tourists. Beatrice should be on television. 'While we are waiting for the peaches to soften, I geeve you a glass of lovely almond amaretto liqueur with its base of apricot kernels.'

'Now you're talking.' Oscar licked his lips, and closed his eyes as the sweet nectar slid down his throat. 'Why is all Italian food so delicious?'

'You like?'

'I like a lot.'

'Now, we mustn't stop our work. We separate five eggs into a bowl. For each egg yolk we measure out some Marsala wine. My Nana's trick is to use an eggshell as a measure. I fill and pour in one eggshell of Marsala to every egg yolk. We add five tablespoons of sugar and wheesk over a bain-marie. This cooks the custard slowly. The bowl mustn't touch the boiling water or we end up with an omelette. It is getting thick and light as a cloud. You all try. It ees too much work for one cook.' They each had a go; there was much banter, and Caroline could see this communal activity would be perfect for tourists. 'Now, take amaretti biscuits, crumble them into bowls and spoon in the peaches. Then we pour our custard the colour of an Italian sunset over the peaches. It ees as simple as that. Here, Nana has spoons. Dip in and try our perfect *zabaglione*.'

'Mmmm,' purred Oscar. 'It's delicious, so light and fluffy.'

'Those crunchy biscuits and the kick from the Marsala are superb.' Kate dipped her spoon in for another try.

'This is a winner, Antonio.' Oscar took off his pinny and sat down to finish his bowl.

'Thank you, Beatrice.' Antonio managed a smile.

Caroline looked at Kate, a successful businesswoman, and quite fancied herself in the same role. Making plans like this and seeing them succeed was very satisfying. If the Canadians liked it, Antonio could roll it out to other guests and start charging. It would increase profits at the hotel and give Beatrice and her lovely mother much-needed extra income.

At that moment, Izzy and Rafaele ran in, covered in dust, with faces red from the sun. 'Can we have some?' they piped up in unison as Nana gave them spoons to try the *zabaglione*. 'Mmmm,' said Izzy, 'this is the best trifle ever.'

'So,' asked Oscar of Rafaele, 'how's the detective work going?'

Rafaele finished off his bowl, then said, 'Very well. See here in my notebook. Izzy and I have marked down all the boats in the bay, when they come and go, and we've checked in the boatyard to discover what sort of person owns each craft. Some are rich. They have staff and big boats that take them to Sorrento and Amalfi for shopping. Others are poor and just go fishing.'

'And you've got a suspect, have you?' Oscar winked at the grown-ups, indulging Rafaele in his desire to become a master detective like Commissario Mazzotta.

'He has, Daddy, don't make fun,' Izzy cried out, protecting her friend.

'We did find something odd, didn't we?'

'Yes we did, and I'm going to tell Commissario Mazzotta as soon as I see him so he can make enquiries.' Rafaele spoke fast, warming to his theme. 'One of the smaller boats yesterday sat in the bay round the coast, as if the people on it wanted to hide. Today, it hasn't moved. It didn't come back to harbour last night like the others. Instead, we saw a man blow up a tiny dinghy and use it to go to the market in Sorrento to get food. We watched him through binoculars; he managed to drop his bag and it was just full of fruit and veg. Other boat owners go to the tourist shops and come back with parcels tied with bows. They buy things like music boxes, not food. The strange thing was, he seemed nervous, not relaxed like a holidaymaker. He looked behind him all the while he was in his vessel, as if worried someone might be searching for him. If I had to describe him I would say he looked suspicious.'

'You have a vivid imagination,' Oscar scoffed.

'He may have something.' Antonio looked alert. 'The Commissario said everything we notice must be reported. Come with me, Rafaele, and we'll phone Cesare right now.' Rafaele looked vindicated and eager to share his news with a real-life detective.

Beatrice prepared coffee and Baci chocolates for everyone, but Caroline was pulled away when her mobile rang. It was Peter. Immediately she felt guilty. They'd spent all morning and lunchtime together but she'd been so tied up with the cookery project she'd barely given him a thought all afternoon.

'You haven't texted or phoned me.' Peter's wounded tones were clipped, not warm and generous as they had been earlier.

'I'm sorry, I've been busy.' She told him animatedly about her new project and how she'd helped pull the Girasole out of trouble, expecting him to congratulate her. Instead, his response was petulant.

'I'm ill, didn't you get my text telling you? You haven't once asked how I am.'

He was right, she hadn't sparked at his mention of feeling off-colour. 'Sorry, darling, what's wrong?'

'I've got sunstroke. I feel sick and headachy. I could do with you coming over and making me feel better.'

Caroline bit her tongue. If he'd listened to her and not spent hours with the roof down this wouldn't have happened. Still, it would be uncharitable to say *I told you so*. She'd hoped later to print off more recipe booklets, but that would have to wait. It was a shame because she was really enjoying her evening at Beatrice's.

'Of course I'll come over.' Reluctantly she made her excuses and left. Peter was staying in a much more expensive hotel than the Girasole, closer to Sorrento town.

When she reached Peter's room, he was lying in bed feeling sorry for himself. 'If you could stroke my forehead that'd make me better, and I'm gasping for a drink of water.'

She filled a glass from the bottle of *acqua frizzante* on the desk. 'I'd like ice in it too, please.'

Caroline pursed her lips. She'd walked past the ice machine in the lobby and would now have to go back down again. By this time she was feeling tired and longing for bed. Tomorrow would be a busy day. She'd need to arrange the borrowing of cutlery, glasses, coffee cups, bowls and cooking utensils from the Girasole's kitchen, and transport them down to Beatrice's house so everything was ready for the cookery class. But Peter wanted to talk, and kept her up past midnight. As Caroline made her way back to the Girasole, exhausted, she couldn't help thinking how much attention Peter needed. Still, she loved him; and if you loved someone, surely nothing was too much trouble?

Caroline was up early next day. She

and Antonio had sweet-talked the Girasole's chef into allowing his precious cutlery, china and glass out of the kitchen, and they were packing things into boxes and onto trolleys. They'd load everything in Antonio's car. It would take two journeys but that was fine.

'Have you heard any news from the kidnappers or Cesare?' Caroline asked.

'No, nothing. I'm on tenterhooks whenever the phone rings.' Antonio sighed. 'Don't carry that, it's too heavy, I'll do it.' He lifted the load as if it were a box of paper plates, not china ones. His muscles tensed under his tanned skin, making Caroline catch her breath. Peter had a body honed at a gym, but Antonio's was more naturally graceful.

Caroline chided herself for looking and covered up by chatting away. 'After this, I've promised to help Beatrice do a nice display of her olive oils. We're going to set up a farmhouse table in the garden, pick flowers, and lay everything on bright white cloths surrounded by freshly-picked lemons. It'll look super. We're also going to do homemade lemonade for the Canadians. It's exciting, isn't it?'

'Everything's exciting when you're around.' They were leaning over a box together, and suddenly she realised how incredibly close they were. Caroline could see the gold specks in his eyes, could see how his deep chestnut hair had bronze lights in it. For a moment the two of them froze. Antonio's look of longing was so intense, his eyes so deep, dark and full of passion as he held her in his gaze. She felt a blush warm its way up her neck and burn into her cheeks like flames. If only he didn't look at her like that; her heart was racing like she'd run a marathon. It didn't help when he made a move towards her. He mustn't, she mustn't! She swallowed hard, knowing she should move away, should break the silence, but she couldn't, she didn't want to. Then a clanging noise struck the air, and she landed back down in reality to hear her phone ring. She grabbed her bag, and blushed even more when she heard Peter's voice.

'Hi babes, have I got a surprise for you today!'

'Erm . . . hello Peter, what sort of surprise?'

'You and I are going to see a real live volcano. We're going up Vesuvius.'

'What? Today? I . . . I can't, I'm busy.'

'Nonsense. I've arranged everything. I've got a taxi booked so I don't have to drive, the roads up there are said to be dodgy. And I've booked a tour guide. What's more, there are a couple of business acquaintances I know here, they're really nice and I've arranged a drink after. I want to show you off, darling. It's all sorted. You'll love it.'

'I would have done,' Caroline tried to hide her annoyance, 'if you hadn't arranged it for today. You could've asked me first.'

'I wanted it to be a surprise. You're on holiday, why can't you enjoy yourself for once? It'll only be the morning, you'll be free this afternoon.'

'I was doing something . . . ' She was going to say *with Antonio*, but caught herself quickly. 'I was doing something down at Beatrice's. I told you last night about the cookery class. I have to get everything ready.'

'You'll have the afternoon. Look, if it helps, I'll come down to the lemon grove this afternoon and give you a hand. Come on, Caroline, please. It's all arranged.'

'Okay,' she agreed reluctantly. It was nice of him to have arranged a surprise and be thinking about her. Still, she had her own things going on, and he hadn't thought for one minute she mightn't be at his beck and call. That old feeling of tension came over her as her chest tightened. Peter had a knack of driving things through, of having his own agenda. He meant well but he simply didn't think. She gritted her teeth as they arranged a time for him to collect her. She'd have to squeeze everything she'd planned into an afternoon instead of doing it in a leisurely fashion, but it couldn't be helped. Besides, if he was prepared to lend a hand, that would make all the difference.

★　★　★

Commissario Mazzotta called to ask Antonio down to his office in town. 'Something very significant has come up, but I can't show you over the phone. Can you come now?'

'Of course, nothing is more important than finding my sister.'

Antonio sped into town and parked at the Police Station. He was led by an officer in a smart uniform, with gold braiding on his shoulder and a white gun holster at his hip, to Cesare Mazzotta's office where he gave the door a sharp knock.

'*Pronto*.'

The Commissario shook Antonio's hand warmly. 'Thank you for coming so soon. I wanted you to know immediately of any developments so you can take them back to your poor sick father. There are two things. Firstly, do you remember the mac with the missing belt? The person who stole the money in Kate's shop was wearing it.'

'Yes.'

'Well, it belonged to a supplier of truffles who had forgotten it at the hotel. We have found it, stuffed in one of the lockers in the kitchen area, which is most strange. But, the other thing we have found is more significant.' The Commissario took two photographs out of a large brown envelope. They were of fingerprints. He put them side by side on his desk. It was plain to see that the swirly patterns in both photos matched.

'This one,' he pointed to the photo on the left, 'was taken from Signora Weston's shop. This one was taken from the envelope which contained the ransom letter about Louisa.'

'But they're the same.'

'Identical. It is a major break-through. From these we can deduce that the person who robbed the shop is the very same one who has kidnapped Louisa.'

8

Antonio shoved the gearstick up to fifth gear as he sped down the perilously steep road. It hugged the cliffside. Little stones rolled away from his screaming wheels and tumbled towards the sea, shooting dust clouds behind him. He was going dangerously fast, but the call from Cesare Mazzotta's office had urged him to come immediately. They were going to make a strike. Cesare had found the kidnappers. Antonio forced the wheel left, then right, swaying in his seat, narrowly missing a motorcyclist. He drove like his life depended on it, the sweat pouring down his back. *Please, please,* he prayed, *let her be alive, let my dear, dear sister be alive and unharmed.*

★　★　★

'Kate, you're a lifesaver. Are you sure I'm not pulling you away from your shop?' Caroline was hot and bothered over in Beatrice's kitchen grabbing lemon halves from what looked like a pile of a hundred at least. She pushed one into an ancient squeezer, pulled the handle, and juice spurted out.

'Not at all,' Kate answered, sleeves rolled up as she halved more lemons and watched Beatrice measuring sugar into jugs. 'I'm enjoying this cooking lark even though it's hard work. I'm sorry Peter left you in the lurch, that was bad of him.'

Caroline was seething. 'If there's one thing I can't stand, it's someone making a promise and not keeping it.' She squished another fruit with gusto, breathing astringent scent through flared nostrils. Working out her anger got the lemons juiced in double-quick time. Beatrice shot Kate a look which seemed to say, *Men! Hah — English or Italian, they're all unreliable.* Caroline gave another defenceless lemon a vicious juicing. 'Peter rang only this morning to ask me out, he didn't give me any warning. He just assumed I'd say yes, and stupidly I did, just because I was flattered. I only agreed because he promised he'd help us, and now he's too darned busy. Can you believe it? Then, to add insult to injury, guess what he said?'

'Go on.'

'He wanted to help us here, but after all, it was 'only a bit of cooking'. It wasn't 'real business' like his stuff.' She grabbed another lemon and stabbed it, making the other two women jump. 'He's shot off to see someone important in Naples. All that after taking up my morning climbing volcanoes and chatting to his lah-di-dah friends. I never want to see Mr and Mrs Warren Barrington-Parkes or their champagne lifestyle again.'

'You didn't like them?'

'They were hideous, all they talked about was money. They showed us the infinity-edge swimming pool and every inch of their posh apartment — I was even expected to ooh and ahh at their rotten broom cupboard. The wife spent ages telling me where they'd bought everything and how much it cost. All I could think of was the work I had to do here. Still, at least with yours and Beatrice's help, we're ready for tomorrow.'

Kate handed her a glass of finished lemonade. 'This will help calm you down.'

'Mmm, that's delicious, and the table looks superb. You really know how to create a stunning display, Beatrice.' Their Italian friend glowed at her words. There were twenty places set at her huge kitchen table and they had put out chairs in the garden so people could sit outside to listen to Antonio's talk.

'Where is Antonio?' asked Kate.

'After he helped me bring extra chairs from the hotel, he had a message about going to see Commissario Mazzotta; he was in a huge rush and shot off. He's desperate for news. I'm waiting for him to ring. Antonio's Mama Valentina is back home, thank goodness, and his grandmother's all settled in. She and Salvatore are comparing illnesses, bless them. Valentina's beside herself about Louisa. It's a terrible worry to have her daughter missing. She was cross at Antonio for not letting her know straight away, but at least we were able to tell her the investigation is continuing apace.'

Later, when the three women were putting out recipe brochures printed by Caroline, they heard rapping at the door. Cesare Mazzotta stood there, tense and serious. Behind him, two other cars screeched to a halt on the quiet road. Policemen in combat gear and chunky bullet-proof vests got out. Cesare was accompanied by Antonio. The Commissario spoke in lowered tones. 'Please go back in, ladies. This is a dangerous situation.'

'Oh, my God.' Caroline, wide-eyed, slapped her hand to her mouth. 'Please don't say something awful has happened to Louisa.'

Antonio stepped forward, casting caution to the wind, and held her tight. 'It's okay; we don't know for certain but Commissario Mazzotta believes she's being held by kidnappers in one of the boats in the bay.'

Hearing the kerfuffle, Rafaele and Izzy came running downstairs. Beatrice grabbed Rafaele who wriggled free. 'I want to come with you, Commissario, to help with some real detective work.'

'That's not possible. Besides, you have already been essential in identifying the boat where we believe Louisa is held. You did good work, Rafaele, very good. I want you all to remain here,' the Commissario commanded. 'They may have guns. Here it is safe, Antonio will look after you.'

The door slammed shut and they heard the police cars pull away in the direction of the boatyard. Rafaele ran into the lounge with Izzy and called out to everyone, 'We can see from here.

Look, the police are stopping and talking to the owner of the boatyard.'

They crowded to look out of the French windows.

'It looks as if they're commandeering one of the private boats.'

'Don't they have any police boats?' asked Rafaele.

'I asked Cesare in the car why they don't approach by sea. He said it was more likely they would be spotted. Setting off in an unmarked speedboat from the bay, they can hide from the kidnappers until they get near their boat. Look, the police are going out now. They're heading towards the boat you suspected, Rafaele.'

Rafaele had grabbed his binoculars. 'That's the man I saw; he's trying to steer away, but the Commissario's boat is faster.'

Beatrice looked terrified. 'I hope there won't be shooting. What can you see, Rafaele?'

'The police have boarded the boat. The man has his hands up. Oh, and wait, there are two girls emerging.'

Antonio grabbed the binoculars. 'The man with his hands up looks like . . . But it can't be.'

'Who?'

'Why, it's Sophia's husband; you know, our waitress at the Girasole. Yes, I'm certain, it's her husband Leonardo.'

'And the girls, can you see the girls?'

'Yes. They are coming out. One is Sophia and the other . . . My God, it is Louisa. Blessed Madonna, she is alive and she looks unharmed.' With that, he broke down, and the others gathered round to hug and comfort him.

★ ★ ★

Caroline and Antonio approached Salvatore and Valentina's suite of rooms with trepidation. They met Commissario Mazzotta pacing outside the door. 'Oh dear,' said Caroline, 'I guess there's going to be a meltdown in there.'

'True.' The Commissario frowned. 'I fear we may have to press charges against Leonardo. He will not talk until you are there, Antonio, as well as your father. He has been a fool and now he is worried about the effect of his actions on Sophia. It's time to get to the bottom of all this.'

Louisa sat on the sofa in her parents' bedroom, her normally coiffured hair unkempt, her eyes red from crying, her mother holding her tight enough to squeeze the air out of her. Caroline went to sit on the other side. Louisa grabbed her hand like her life depended on it.

In a chair close by sat Sophia, sobbing. She looked up at her hand-cuffed husband who stood, head down, between two uniformed policemen. As soon as Antonio entered, he flung open the balcony doors to let some air into the charged atmosphere.

'What on earth were you thinking, man?' boomed Salvatore.

'Please try not to shout, my love, the situation is difficult enough as it is.' Valentina stroked her daughter's hand.

'I am finding it difficult to contain my temper. This man has put us through hell. Not just our family but his own wife.'

'Mr di Labati,' said Cesare Mazzotta, trying to take the heat out of the situation, 'perhaps it would be useful to hear from the culprits. So, whose idea was this whole sorry charade?'

'It was mine,' Leonardo piped up. 'My wife had nothing to do with it. The blame is all mine and I am sorry. Truly sorry, everything got out of hand.' Sophia sobbed quietly. 'Commissario, Senor di Labati, we were desperate. I bought that stupid boat when I was doing well. I wanted to impress my friends. I wish to goodness now I'd never seen it. Suddenly, without warning, jobs were cut, I was made redundant and I couldn't find work. Then, Sophia fell pregnant.'

Sophia butted in, 'I couldn't tell you, Mr di Labati. I was being sick all the time, I thought I would get the sack too. Our creditors came knocking on the door and no-one wanted to buy the boat. It was me who did the first bad thing. I stole money from Senora Weston's shop.'

Salvatore waded in with a face like thunder. 'And threatened the entire business of my beautiful hotel. Just when I was ill and least able to deal with things. Then your feckless husband goes and kidnaps my only daughter. How could he? How could you jeopardize the hotel that has given you work?' His face became redder. The walls of the room vibrated with his anger.

Louisa stood up on shaky legs and placed a hand on her father's shoulder. 'Papa, please take care. It was a horrible experience, but right from the start I knew that Leonardo would not harm me. He was trying to be head of his family, like you, except he is not so good at it. Sophia kept on telling him to give himself up. They were desperate, both of them. Sophia stole the money because she didn't know what else to do. If you hadn't confiscated my phone, I might have been able to get in touch and ask for help. Being kept against my will on the boat, I had a lot of time to think and speculate about what I would do if I was in their situation. I wonder, if we were all faced with having no money, big debts, no jobs and another mouth to feed, if we wouldn't also do foolish things, then worry about the consequences later. Leonardo didn't know you were ill, nor Sophia. They both did awful things, but Sophia knew nothing of the kidnap until Leonardo bundled me on the boat. She was suffering ghastly morning sickness and was there recuperating. She pleaded with Leonardo to take me back, but by then he was in too deep, and she was terrified about having stolen from Kate's shop. Papa, Commissario, it wasn't Sophia who wrote the ransom letter, despite her fingerprints being on the envelope. You see, Leonardo isn't even a good enough criminal to make sure he doesn't implicate his wife by mistake. He just grabbed one of her envelopes from home to scribble the ransom note. I hated Leonardo at first, I would have happily shot him if I had a gun. But then I came to pity him. I realized this sorry mess is what people who have nothing fall into. This dreadful experience has at least taught me what is important in life. We have so much, and they have so little.'

Valentina's eyes brimmed with tears at her daughter's words. She glanced at Leonardo. At every sentence, Leonardo's head seemed further weighed down with shame and misery. He looked less like a hardened criminal, and more like a broken man. But Salvatore still simmered with rage, jabbing his finger accusingly towards Leonardo.

'I will deal with you in a moment. I beg your pardon, Commissario, for taking over, but please could you tell me exactly what evidence there is against Sophia. I expect all my employees to be loyal and clearly she has not fulfilled that role.'

The Commissario consulted his notebook. 'One of the tourists whose money was stolen had noted down all the serial numbers of the euro notes. When one of them turned up in a local shop, Sophia's fingerprints were on the stolen money. Although she is guilty of this, I do not think she was involved in the kidnapping.'

Sophia looked up at both men pleadingly. 'I am so sorry. I used that mac that the truffle supplier left behind by mistake, and I padded myself out and wore sunglasses as a disguise. It was awful of me, but I needed cash so badly. I only spent it on baby clothes and a pram for my baby.'

Salvatore's eyes narrowed. 'I believe you. Your crime was bad enough. But you,' he pointed to Leonardo, 'you are much worse. You took from me one of my most precious things — Louisa. When you have a child of your own you will realise how appalling a crime that is, how it eats at the very heart of a father. I was convinced that old goat Casiraghi was at the centre of all this. I was ready to have it out with him; think of the trouble that would have made.'

The air was heavy as they all considered the implications of an escalation in the fight between the two old rivals. Then, her voice breaking, Louisa spoke. 'If only Mama had been here, I think maybe none of this would have happened. She talks to everyone, she looks after the staff as well as her own family. Maybe Sophia would have confessed her problems to Mama and things wouldn't have got out of hand.'

At this, Sophia broke down, sobbing. Leonardo lunged forward to comfort her but was firmly held back by the two policemen. Sophia cried out, 'What is going to happen to us?'

Caroline handed Louisa and Sophia fresh tissues. She felt sorry for everyone. Antonio was pacing the room, looking as livid as his father. Someone had to step in and try and pour oil on troubled waters. Caroline took a deep breath. She might be shot down in flames but she was going to say what she thought if it killed her. 'They did wrong, Salvatore, but in England we have a phrase, 'two wrongs don't make a right'. I assume, Commissario, that Leonardo will definitely be charged with kidnapping.'

'Yes, it's a very serious crime.'

'But perhaps whether Sophia is arrested depends upon whether Salvatore wishes to press charges.'

'That is true. If Salvatore wishes not to press charges, we will respect his decision.'

At that moment, Valentina's mother, who had been sitting quietly in the corner, got up and came over to her son-in-law. She said some quiet words to Salvatore in Italian.

'What did she say?' asked Caroline, appealing to Antonio.

Antonio looked steadily at Salvatore as he said, 'She told my father that we all make mistakes, particularly when we are young, and that if people don't forgive us it can end in tragedy. She doesn't want an indiscretion to lead to a disaster. I believe she is thinking of her own actions in the war and how she nearly had that airman killed. She has been forgiven and she wants forgiveness for Sophia. Her husband will have to do his time in jail, but my grandmother is thinking of their baby.'

They looked at Salvatore. His body language had subtly changed. His chest was no longer puffed out, his brows no longer knitted in anger. He threw his hands up in true Italian style. He realized that it would make him more of a man to forgive than to prosecute. '*Mamma mia.* You women are a force to be reckoned with. I realize,' he said slowly, 'that I am a lucky man. I have a clever son, a loving wife, a beautiful daughter and a mother-in-law who is wiser than all the saints. We can all learn, however young or old — I too can learn to forgive.' With a supreme effort he squeezed the next words out. 'I . . . I love you my daughter, even more now that I nearly lost you. Terrible though it has been, this experience has made you grow up. To hear you speak with so much compassion and thought for others has melted my heart.'

He turned to Sophia. 'You can keep the baby things you have bought. I cannot begrudge you those. Leonardo, it is a very difficult thing being head of a family. You have a lot to learn, and you must pay for what you did. But I forgive your wife, and there will be a job for her here at the Girasole after she has her baby, so that she can support the little one until you are free. Maybe if the two of you are given some good luck, you will be able to put your lives back together.'

'Thank you,' Sophia and Leonardo said before they were led out of the room by the police.

'Oh Papa.' Louisa ran into his arms. 'Let's put this behind us. We are together again, all of us. *La famiglia* is what is important, and the fact that we love each other and will never be parted again.'

★ ★ ★

The next day, the Canadians swarmed over the Lemon Grove like bees. The cookery demonstration was a runaway success, and everyone pronounced the *zabaglione* to be heaven on a spoon. 'Look at these darling trees with real lemons, Harman, did you ever see anything like it? They're so huge.'

'The lemonade is delicious, ain't it, sweetie? I must get the recipe.'

Beatrice was in her element. She'd laid out a table with her whole range so people could taste the varied quality of the different bottles of her olive oil. Chunks of fresh ciabatta bread had been cut by Rafaele's Nana, and the Canadians dipped them in the oils to taste whilst Beatrice explained, 'This bottle ees the first pressing. It produces the sweetest, fruitiest oil. We call that extra-virgin olive oil. Then we have *fino*, and finally light.'

'I'll have three bottles to take back,' piped up one of the Canadians, 'and throw me in three bottles of that limoncello liqueur.' Beatrice and Nana could barely keep up; their pockets were stuffed with euros.

Antonio and Caroline took their cups of coffee down to the end of the lemon grove to look at La Casa. It was all finished now, looking spruce and perfect, with the waves lapping at the rocks outside the front garden. It was heavenly. Caroline would miss Italy when she left; and, she had to admit, she would miss Antonio too. So very much. The gentle breeze lifted his fringe, the clear bright sun blonded the hairs on his arms. How would it be when she had to say goodbye? She simply couldn't imagine the scene. It would be like seeing snow falling on the hot sand, or watching a waterfall flow upwards. It was inconceivable. She felt her lip tremble and turned away.

Tomorrow, she was to book her

flights back home. She had delayed, but Peter was pressing her and she knew she must do it. They had talked about buying a flat in London. All that concrete and glass would be a million miles away from the sighing sea and the gentle wind which kissed the leaves of the lemon trees. And life with Peter would be . . . different. True, he had made an effort, and it was clear he really loved her, but she had to admit Peter called the shots in any relationship. She must accept that. What's more, Peter was already a little bit married to his work. She was sure that would all readjust after the wedding. He'd change his priorities, even though success in his world was measured in terms of money. Of course he'd make their marriage the centre of his world, especially when they had children.

'You will come back and visit, won't you?' Antonio's soft tones broke the silence.

'Of course,' she promised, but sadness tinged her tones. She would be a married woman then. Would Peter want to stay in the humble house on the beach, or would he prefer the expensive hotel which she found cold and unrelaxing? She bit her lip and said again, 'Of course, I could never get enough of Italy. In fact, I'm visiting Pompeii again tomorrow.'

'You are?'

'Yes. Peter wants to see it.'

'Ahh. There is so much to enjoy, however many times I go I never get bored. By the way, with everything that has been going on, I didn't tell you; my Professore phoned. He wants to give me a job at Pompeii after all. The young American's father has cancelled the funding he promised. His business has got into financial trouble in the recession and he is no longer quite the hotshot he was.'

'But I thought that for the final dig and the extra work to take place they had to have that funding.'

'My Professore is a wily old bird. As soon as he heard hints Rick McPartlin's father was in trouble, he got in touch with his competitors and they were only too happy to move in and fill the gap. It is a game of one-upmanship.'

'Oh, Antonio, I'm so pleased.'

'But I shall have to turn it down.'

'Why?'

'My father needs me full-time at the Girasole now more than ever. I cannot have him getting stressed and ill again.'

'That's awful. To have your dream so close but then so far.'

'I have come to terms with it. In life there are many dreams which don't come true.' For a second he looked at her longingly, then said with finality, 'Come, I hear Beatrice calling us for coffee.'

★ ★ ★

The next day dawned bright with sky the colour of forget-me-nots. Caroline was waiting in the Girasole's driveway for Peter to arrive to take her to Pompeii. The air was like champagne. It retained the last vestiges of night-time coolness before the heat started to warm the stone wall she leant on, and bake the tiny flowers growing out of it. Caroline was thoughtful. At breakfast, Mel had told her she had turned down Cesare, for now at least.

Caroline had been stunned. 'But why? He's such a lovely guy.'

'He is. It's just too soon for me to settle down. I still have the travel bug I had when I was younger. Coming out here to Italy, seeing different ways of life, has made me want to travel just one more time before I settle down. Cesare says he'll wait for me, and maybe finally then I will be ready.'

'That's sad. I think you'd make a wonderful couple.'

'I have to be certain, though, Caroline. It would be unfair unless I was one hundred percent sure.'

Caroline was still musing over their conversation when Peter arrived. In the car, he chatted about work, for which Caroline was grateful. There were so many things buzzing through her head she couldn't concentrate on small talk. Then his words pulled her out of her reverie. 'Oh, and you have booked your tickets home, haven't you?'

'I will.'

'Don't worry, I'll book them for you.'

'Really, Peter, I can do it myself.'

'It's no problem, let me sort it.' She felt a bristle of annoyance run up her spine. 'I've got a great travel agent, he'll sort it. You just relax.'

When they reached Pompeii, he'd pre-booked a tour guide. Caroline had been looking forward to buying a book in the gift shop and going around just the two of them, looking at the things she had missed when here with Antonio. Had Peter asked her she would have vehemently objected to a guided tour. The man was stilted and she found herself yawning as he reeled out in a bored voice information he'd said a hundred times before to a thousand other tourists. This was worlds away from the fabulous time she'd had with Antonio. Peter held her hand tightly. Instead of wanting his touch like she had when Antonio had gathered her into his arms, her fingers felt crushed as if Peter's hold was a ball and chain restricting her.

'You're quiet,' said Peter on the drive back. 'I guess it's because those old crusty monuments are pretty boring, aren't they?'

'Peter, you're going too fast. Please slow down. And no, Pompeii is not boring, it's fascinating. You just have to see it in the right circumstances.' Peter revved up the car and overtook two others on a blind bend. 'Peter, please. I've asked you to slow down.'

His jaw was set, firm and unyielding. 'What do you mean, *in the right circumstances?* Surely you mean 'with the right person'? I suppose you're talking about that Italian bloke. I knew there was something going on between you.'

She stared at him. 'There is *nothing* going on between me and Antonio. As soon as I knew you were coming to Italy — and let's not forget you and I were finished when I first came out here, the engagement was off — I kept as clear of Antonio's company as I could. I've spent loads of time with you.'

'But you continued with those ridiculous cooking lessons just to be with him.'

'No. I did that because it's a great business idea, and I've got a brain I want to use and things *I* want to do. And they are *not* ridiculous. That's always been the trouble with you Peter. You want a lapdog, not a girlfriend or a wife.'

Peter screeched to a halt at some traffic lights, narrowly avoiding going through them. They were right by Castellammare di Stabia train station.

'Don't be foolish. I admit I want a proper wife. I want someone who cares for me and listens to me.'

'I do care for you Peter. But you want someone who does what they're told and follows meekly in your shadow. I'm sorry Peter, that's not me. I'm independent, I make my own decisions, and I'm making one right now. I'm getting out of here. I'm going back to Sorrento by train. Sorry Peter.' She reached out, held his hand briefly knowing it would be for the last time, then let it go and thrust open the car door. 'It's over. I can never be the woman you need. I hope you find someone lovely, but I'm not the woman for you. This time we really are *finished*.'

'Please, Caroline think again — '

'We'd spend a lifetime arguing. Sorry.'

'At least let me take you back, don't leave like this.'

She knew, if she got back in that car, it might give him the chance to persuade her away from her decision. This was one of life's turning points. She'd made up her mind. 'It's best, Peter. I need fresh air. I think we both need to calm down.' She turned, and as she walked away it was suddenly as if a great weight had been lifted from her shoulders. The hold Peter had on her was over, once and for all. She was free.

★   ★   ★

The next morning, she woke up early at the Girasole, showered, and desperately needed a walk to clear her head before breakfast. She really should book her flight back today. La Casa — Oscar and Izzy's house on the beach — was finished and looking beautiful. There was no reason to stay in Sorrento any longer. Slipping on yellow shorts, a white t-shirt and flip-flops, she wandered out of the hotel and down the winding road towards the beach. In the distance she could hear the familiar sounds of the Girasole getting ready to greet its guests. The tinkle of cutlery on china, one of the chefs singing an old Neapolitan love song in a vibrant baritone. Italy had worked its way into her blood, it was written like a poem on her heart.

Passing the lemon grove, she waved cheerily to Rafaele's Nana, who was always up at dawn and sat by the window shelling peas. As she turned the bend, Caroline stood, hands in pockets. There, glowing in the morning sun, was La Casa di Spiaggia, looking like an oil painting done by an old master. Izzy and Oscar would come here over the years and she would share good times with them. Izzy's children, in decades to come, would jump off the rocks into the sea. Oscar and Kate, if they stayed together, would toast many an Italian sunset in sparkling Prosecco. Surely even Mel would come back here to visit once she had finished her travels round the world.

Suddenly, the front door opened and Caroline's face lit up to see Antonio.

Antonio thought the figure standing there up on the road looking wistfully down was Caroline. Had she come to say goodbye to La Casa? The joy he always felt at seeing her was tinged with a hollow feeling of dread. Her flight would be booked back to London. Maybe by now she would even have a date for her wedding to the Englishman. Antonio waved and beckoned her down. More beautiful than ever in the soft morning light, she had not a scrap of makeup on her clear skin. She asked, 'Antonio, what are you doing here?'

'Signor Ponti left the keys in the door for me so I could water in these plants. We had some left over from remodelling the Girasole's garden, so I thought I'd put them here as a thank-you for all you have done for us. The window boxes now have trailing red geraniums, and there is white jasmine to climb over the door. Pink bougainvillea at the back will grow up the hillside and frame La Casa. I hope Oscar and Izzy like them.'

'They're lovely. Even more so because you planted them.'

It was as if she had stabbed Antonio in the heart. He wished she wouldn't say sweet things like that. After all, he was nothing to her and never could be. She had the arrogant Englishman who possessed her, like she was a tropical bird in a gilded cage.

He sat down on the wrought-iron bench outside La Casa's front door looking out to sea. The bay was as calm as a looking-glass. A slight plop in the distance signalled a fish gulping at the surface and diving back into the crystal blue depths. A crowd of chattering sparrows flew noisily past. 'All of this will feel very tame to you back in London. I guess you've missed all the excitement of a big city.'

'Not at all.' Caroline placed herself beside him. She was closer than normal. She had no idea what passions she aroused in him. 'This place has meant more to me than I'd ever have guessed. It's helped me find myself. I was a little lost when I came here.'

And now she has Peter back in her world, he thought dejectedly. She had found her future and she was leaving to start a new life. Antonio gazed at her, drinking her in. Her eyes this morning were unbelievable, so clear and bright, her lips rose red, her skin glowed like the pearls in the ocean. She was perfect. She was someone else's. 'There will always be a place for you here Caroline. And there will always be somebody here for you.'

'Somebody. What do you mean?'

He turned to her; he was about to make a fool of himself, all caution thrown to the wind. He grasped her hands in his and brought them to his lips. 'I know you've made up your mind, you're going to live with him, and I wish you the best of luck. But, darling Caroline, if things don't work out, if you change your mind, I am here for you. I will always be. Do you understand what I'm saying?'

He imagined she would pull away. He feared she might even wrench her hands out of his and run like a rabbit, scared of his passion. But she didn't. Amazingly, she brought her hand up to his forehead, ran her fingers through the thick fringe which he had hidden behind. His heart pounded, he could feel it thumping against his chest. 'I think I do. And I think you should know that I'm not going with Peter.'

'Now it is me who does not understand,' he stuttered, searching in her eyes for the truth.

'We've split up. For good. This time it's over.'

There was silence. Antonio couldn't believe what he was hearing. Now was his chance. 'Would you stay, Caroline? If I asked you, would you stay, in Sorrento with me so I can be here for you, take care of you?' He could feel hope rising in him like a tidal wave.

'I might. On one condition.'

'Which is?'

'That you take that job at Pompeii. I'll help run the hotel, if your father will let me. You and I can help him together. I . . . well, if you don't mind me hanging around here for a while, I'd be happy to stay. Just here. Just the two of us. The thing is,' she looked down nervously, her hands wrapping tightly over one another, 'I realize it's you I love, Antonio. I think I have for a long time. I only *thought* I was in love with Peter, but it wasn't true love, not giving, caring love.'

Antonio had never felt exultation, but he did now. He cradled her face in his hands, '*Cara mia*, don't just stay for a while, stay forever. I love you. I couldn't live without you. You stole my heart the first day I saw you by the pool. I am yours, my beautiful English girl, for as long as you want me, and only yours.' And with that, he took her in a kiss which lasted a lifetime, as they entwined around one another as surely as the newly planted jasmine would wrap itself around La Casa di Spiaggia, brightening its days in the fierce heat of many an Italian summer to come.

VALENTINE MASQUERADE

Margaret Sutherland

New Year's Eve is hot and sultry in more ways than one when a tall, handsome prince fixes the newest lady in his court with a magnetic gaze. Who could say no to a prince — especially a charmer like Will Bradshaw? Caitlin has to wonder. And Will wonders, too, if he might have finally found the woman to banish the hurts of years gone by. But what if the one ill-judged mistake of Caitlin's past happens to be the single fault he can't accept?

THE HOUSE ON THE HILL

Miranda Barnes

When a young man moves into the old house next door, Kate Jackson's curiosity is piqued. However, handsome Elek Costas is suspiciously reclusive, and the two get off to a bad start when he accuses her of trespassing. Whilst Kate is dubious of Elek's claim to be the rightful owner, her boyfriend Robert has his eye on acquiring the property for himself . . . Just what is the mystery of Hillside House? Kate is determined to find out!